Alice-Miranda

Takes the Stage

JACQUELINE HARVEY

DELACORTE PRESS

All rights reserved. Published in the United States by Delacorte Press, an imprint of
Random House Children's Books, a division of Random House, Inc., New York.
Originally published in paperback by Random House Australia, a division of the
Random House Group, Sydney, in 2010.

Delacorte Press is a registered trademark and the colophon is a
trademark of Random House, Inc.

Visit us on the Web! randomhouse.com/kids

Educators and librarians, for a variety of teaching tools, visit us at
RHTeachersLibrarians.com

Library of Congress Cataloging-in-Publication Data
Harvey, Jacqueline.
[Alice-Miranda takes the lead]
Alice-Miranda takes the stage / Jacqueline Harvey. — First American edition.
pages cm
Summary: "There's loads of drama in store for Alice-Miranda and her friends at
boarding school"—Provided by publisher.
ISBN 978-0-385-74333-4 (hc) — ISBN 978-0-375-99107-3 (glb) —
ISBN 978-0-449-81074-3 (ebook) [1. Boarding schools—Fiction. 2. Schools—Fiction.
3. Theater—Fiction.] I. Title.
PZ7.H2674785Ao 2013
[Fic]—dc23
2012025725

The text of this book is set in 12-point Century Schoolbook.

Printed in the United States of America

10 9 8 7 6 5 4 3 2 1

First American Edition

For Ian and Sandy

For Linsay and Kimberley

room!" Miss Grimm smiled and plonked herself down in the striped armchair beside the fireplace in her study. Dressed casually in jeans and a pretty orange shirt, Ophelia Grimm was the picture of happiness.

The girls exchanged quizzical looks and then disintegrated into fits of giggles. Mr. Grump, who was sitting in the armchair opposite, roared with laughter.

"You should have seen those poor monkeys." Aldous Grump grinned at his new wife. "They didn't have a hope with Ophelia after them. Ran for their lives, they did—thought they'd be better off taking their chances with the lions out on the game reserve."

"Very funny, darling," Miss Grimm admonished. "I was just tired of the little brutes raiding my makeup purse, that's all. I hadn't realized chimps were fond of lipstick and blush until I caught them giving each other a makeover at the dressing table after we returned from breakfast one morning."

"We must have stayed at the same lodge when we were on safari last year," said Alice-Miranda, "because the very same thing happened to Mummy. The manager, Mr. Van Rensburg, said that his chimps had collected enough stolen lipstick to start their own beauty parlor. Apart from that, it does sound like you had a lovely time."

"We most certainly did." Mr. Grump nodded.

Chapter 1

Twelve pairs of eyes widened in unison, awaiting Miss Ophelia Grimm's next move. She stood in the corner of the room, a scarlet flush creeping up from her neck to her cheeks. Her blond hair sparked with static and her lips drew tightly together.

"Out!" Her shrill voice shattered the silence. "Get out and don't come back, you horrid little monsters!"

Eleven girls reeled backward in terror, their hands clutching pallid faces. Millie's cinnamon freckles turned white and Jacinta's mouth gaped open. Only Alice-Miranda dared to smile.

"And that, my dears, was how I got rid of the two cheeky chimps who had taken up residence in our

Alice-Miranda

Takes the Stage

Also by Jacqueline Harvey

Alice-Miranda at School
Alice-Miranda on Vacation

Millie took the last sip of her hot chocolate, up-ended the delicate blue-and-white mug and allowed a sodden marshmallow to slide into her mouth.

"Mmm, yum!" she exclaimed.

"All done?" Miss Grimm asked.

Millie nodded.

"Well, girls, I think you had better be heading off. School tomorrow, and we have loads of exciting things planned for the term." Miss Grimm stood up and walked toward the mahogany door.

"But can't we stay and hear more?" Jacinta grumbled. "I want to know what happened to the baby elephant you saw on safari. Did he escape from that crocodile?"

"Next time," Miss Grimm promised. "And, girls?" She tapped her finger to her cheek as though she had just remembered something important. "We have a new student starting tomorrow. She'll be rooming with you, Jacinta, so I expect you to make her feel *very* welcome." Ophelia arched her eyebrow and gave Jacinta a meaningful look.

Jacinta nodded like a jack-in-the-box.

"A new girl? That's lovely," Alice-Miranda replied. "I can't wait to meet her. What's her name?"

"Sloane. Sloane Sykes," Miss Grimm replied. "Now, off you go, girls."

Alice-Miranda was the first to stand. She said goodnight to Mr. Grump, who was still sitting in his armchair. Without warning, the tiny child leaned forward and gave him a peck on his stubbly cheek.

"Now, what was that for?" Aldous asked.

"Just because," Alice-Miranda replied, before skipping over to Miss Grimm to give her a warm hug too. Miss Grimm smiled at her youngest student with the cascading chocolate curls and eyes as big as saucers.

"And you know something?" Alice-Miranda scanned the walls on either side of the door. "I simply love your photographs. That one of you and Mr. Grump is gorgeous, and that one of the elephant is too cute—you could enter it in a competition."

The previously bare walls now played host to more than a dozen pictures: Miss Grimm and Mr. Grump's wedding, their honeymoon and even some casual shots of Miss Grimm with girls around the school. There were faces and places and memories.

"Do you remember, Miss Grimm, when I first met you, I said that what this room needed was some photographs? And now look—it's perfect!"

"Yes, young lady, I certainly do recall that was one of your recommendations, among rather a few others," Miss Grimm teased. Alice-Miranda grinned

{4}

and leaned forward to give the headmistress another quick hug.

The group of girls behind her took turns saying goodnight to Miss Grimm and Mr. Grump. It was amazing how much things had changed at Winchesterfield-Downsfordvale in the past few months. Who would ever have thought that Alice-Miranda Highton-Smith-Kennington-Jones, along with eleven of her friends, would enjoy an hour in the headmistress's study, hearing all about her recent honeymoon safari in Africa?

Alice-Miranda smiled to herself. She couldn't wait to see what excitement the new term would bring.

Chapter 2

Alice-Miranda led the charge across the cobble-stoned courtyard toward Grimthorpe House. From her position on the dimly lit veranda, the house mistress, Mrs. Howard, peered out into the darkness, a flurry of bother frothing on her lips.

"Oh, thank heavens!" she exclaimed. "I was worrying myself into an early grave. Where on earth have you been? Dinner was an hour ago. Now hurry up inside. It's cool out, and the last thing I need is a house full of coughs and splutters."

The girls poured into the hallway, one after the other. Mrs. Howard gathered them around her like a mother hen, locked the front door and turned to face her charges.

"Sorry, Mrs. Howard, we should have phoned you," Alice-Miranda began. "Miss Grimm and Mr. Grump invited us back to the study for hot chocolate and marshmallows and we lost track of the time. Miss Grimm was telling us about their honeymoon in Africa. It all sounded so wonderful. They went on a safari and they saw elephants and lions and hippos—"

"And guess what, Howie?" Millie interrupted as she rushed through from behind Alice-Miranda. "Two monkeys invaded their bedroom and stole Miss Grimm's lipstick and when she was telling us about it, I almost jumped out of my skin. She's good at scary stories, that's for sure."

Mrs. Howard rolled her eyes. "Imagine that! Well, run along, girls and brush your teeth. I'll be in to turn the lights off in ten minutes."

The girls began to disappear through doorways along opposite sides of the long corridor. Alice-Miranda and Millie were headed toward their room when Jacinta whispered Millie's name. She then opened and closed her hands, signaling the number ten. "Ten minutes. Okay?" Jacinta asked.

Millie gave two thumbs up.

"What was that fo–?" Alice-Miranda began. Millie promptly put her hand over Alice-Miranda's mouth and gave her a gentle shove into their bedroom.

Millie shut the door and flopped down onto her bed. "Midnight meeting in Jacinta's room."

"Midnight! What fun! But it's school tomorrow," Alice-Miranda said as she unbuttoned her shirt. "Won't that upset Mrs. Howard? I don't think she was very happy about our staying out late tonight." She retrieved her pajamas from under her pillow and began to get changed.

"Don't worry about Howie," Millie replied. "She was just pretending to be annoyed. She could have phoned the kitchen if she was *that* worried. Anyway, the girls on the corridor always have a 'midnight meeting' on the first night back."

"We didn't last term," Alice-Miranda replied.

Millie explained that this was because Alethea wouldn't allow anyone except *her* friends last term. Apparently the meeting was not really at midnight anyway, more like quarter to nine, and usually someone fell asleep by quarter past and everyone got off to bed by ten at the latest. After vacations, when the girls got to stay up later, it was hard to go back to the routine of eight-thirty bedtime for at least a couple of nights.

"We can talk about what we did over vacation," Millie informed her friend.

"But, Millie, there are some things we *can't* talk about from vacation," Alice-Miranda reminded her.

During the school vacation, Alice-Miranda, Jacinta and Millie had far more adventure and excitement than any of them had bargained for. Jacinta had gone to stay with Alice-Miranda for the whole break. The two girls quickly found themselves at the mercy of a rather cranky boy and a dastardly stranger. When Millie arrived to join in the fun for Aunt Charlotte's birthday party, things went from bad to worse. A case of mistaken identity saw dear old Aunty Gee kidnapped by a gang of rogues intent on getting their hands on the Highton-Smith-Kennington-Joneses' cook and her formula for Just Add Water Freeze-Dried Foods. The fact that Mrs. Oliver and Aunty Gee looked like twins had a lot to do with the confusion. In the end Aunty Gee returned safely and Alice-Miranda's bravery ensured that the crooks were captured, but the girls had been sworn to secrecy. Since Aunty Gee also happened to be the Queen, her future freedom depended on their

{9}

silence. Indeed, she would never be allowed anywhere on her own again if news of such misadven-
tures reached the palace.

"Do we take snacks?" Alice-Miranda asked. "Because Mrs. Oliver packed a whole tin of her chocolate fudge."

"Yum." Millie licked her lips. "Treats are always
welcome. But don't expect to have any leftovers."

Alice-Miranda and Millie finished changing into
their pajamas, grabbed their toothbrushes and hurried to the bathroom at the end of the hallway. The
place was a hive of activity as all of the girls from the
ground floor readied themselves for bed.

Not five minutes later, the bathroom was empty
and Mrs. Howard was patroling the corridor, poking
her head into each room, saying her goodnights and
flicking off the lights.

Alice-Miranda and Millie lay in the dark, watching
the clock as the minutes ticked by slowly until eight-
forty-five.

"It's time," Millie whispered as she pushed back
the covers and sat up, swiveling her legs around to
scoop her slippers from the floor.

Alice-Miranda hopped out of bed and pulled on her
bathrobe, then slid her feet into her pink slippers.
"This is such fun!" She smiled. Her tummy was full

of butterflies. "Are you sure Mrs. Howard won't mind?"

"Trust me," Millie replied. "It's a first night tradition. Well, most of the time." She grabbed Alice-Miranda's tiny hand and they scampered to the door.

Chapter 3

The corridor was empty. Alice-Miranda followed her friend as they tiptoed along the softly lit hall to Jacinta's door. Other doors were opening, and it wasn't long before there were at least ten other girls headed to the same place.

"Password?" Jacinta's voice murmured on the other side of the door.

"Dead," Millie replied, louder than she had intended.

"That's not it," Jacinta whispered back.

"No, but that's what you'll be if you don't hurry up and let us in," Millie threatened.

Jacinta giggled and opened the door.

The stream of visitors poured into the room, finding themselves comfortable spots on Jacinta's bed and the spare bed that was to be Sloane Sykes's as of tomorrow. Alice-Miranda and Millie sat cross-legged on the Persian rug in the middle of the timber floor and Alice-Miranda offered the fudge tin around.

Just as the group got settled there was a shuffling sound outside the room, followed by a booming voice.

"Jacinta Headlington-Bear, turn off that light, or I will be in to turn it off for you," Mrs. Howard instructed. The girls froze. Jacinta had left her bedside lamp on so everyone could see their way in.

"Just doing it now, Howie," Jacinta called back.

The girls remained silent until they heard the house mistress's footsteps on the stairs at the end of the hall.

"That was close," Susannah whispered as the group let out a collective breath.

Jacinta grabbed her flashlight from the bedside table, held it under her chin and flicked on the switch, doing her best impression of a ghost. "Welcome to Grimthorpe Hoooooouse." Everyone giggled.

"So what do we want to talk about?" Danika asked.

Now that she was officially Head Prefect she thought she had better take the lead. "What did everyone do over vacation?"

Ivory, Shelby and Ashima all complained about having to stay at home and being totally bored.

"Well, I saw Alethea," Susannah began. "She was walking out of Highton's in the city with her mother and she almost knocked me over."

"Please, can we talk about more *pleasant* things?" Lizzy replied as she glanced at Shelby and Danika. The three girls had once been Alethea's best friends until they realized how incredibly horrid she was.

Alethea Goldsworthy had been Head Prefect at the beginning of the year, until it was revealed that she was a cheat and a liar, and she had consequently left the school in a terrible hurry. She had treated Alice-Miranda especially badly.

"Well, I feel sorry for her," said Alice-Miranda.

Millie turned to her. "Why? She's totally evil. And after what she did to you, she deserved everything she got."

"I'm sure she's not mean and awful all the time," Alice-Miranda replied.

"You're too nice, Alice-Miranda, that's your problem," said Ivory, smiling at her little friend.

"No, I'm not." Alice-Miranda shook her head.

"No, she's *really* not," Jacinta agreed. "You should have seen what she did to Mr. Blu–" Millie and Alice-Miranda shot Jacinta a stare that would halt a river of lava. "Oh, never mind."

Danika practically pounced on Jacinta. "What were you about to say?"

"Nothing, nothing at all," Jacinta lied. "Umm, does anyone know where that secret passage is off the science room?"

The girls shook their heads.

"Don't you remember Alethea saying that she'd found a secret passage but she was the only one allowed to go there?" Jacinta continued.

"Knowing Alethea, she was probably just showing off," Lizzy said. "But we should look for it. You never know—maybe she was telling the truth for once in her life."

"O-o-o-o-h-a-a-a-h." Alice-Miranda yawned and rubbed her eyes. "Sorry, I'm really tired. I might go to bed."

"No!" Jacinta wailed. "It's too early. I know, let's tell ghost stories."

Millie clasped her hands together. "I love ghost stories."

"No, not ghost stories," said Madeline, shaking her head. "I think we should tell Alice-Miranda a true story—about the witch in the woods."

"A witch in the woods?" Alice-Miranda frowned. "What do you mean?"

"I suppose we never got around to telling you about her last term because there were too many other things going on," Madeline began. "But now you *need* to know."

"Definitely . . . yes . . . for sure," the other girls chorused, nodding their heads.

"But I don't believe in witches." Alice-Miranda smiled. "They're only in fairy stories."

"Well, you should believe this—because it's absolutely true." Susannah wriggled forward to the edge of the bed. "Come and sit up here next to me." She patted the bedspread.

The youngest child stood up and moved in beside Susannah and Ashima on the bed. Millie stayed on the floor looking up at the storyteller.

"All right, you'd better start at the beginning," Alice-Miranda directed.

"Well." Susannah lowered her voice. "In the woods not far from here, there's a witch. She lives on her own in a gigantic house overgrown with vines and hidden by the forest. There's no one there except her and about a hundred cats, all meowing and calling and scratching and fighting."

The girls began to shift uncomfortably. Alice-Miranda's brown eyes were wide.

"Have you seen her?" Alice-Miranda asked. "I mean, anyone could make that up. Some of the children who live at Highton Mill, the village near our place, probably tell the same stories about Granny Bert—and she's not scary at all."

"I disagree! She's mad," Jacinta disputed.

Madeline leaned over and took the flashlight from Jacinta, and held it under her chin. "This witch is tall, possibly the tallest woman you'll ever meet, and she has enormous hands like a man and she wears the same black clothes every day and her teeth, well, the ones she has, are rotten and crooked and there's a fang . . ."

The girls were now on the edge of the bed leaning in toward the storyteller.

"But the worst thing is her face," Madeline whispered. "It's . . ." Madeline grabbed her cheeks and pulled one up and one down, splaying the flesh between her fingers.

At that same moment, a branch scratched against the window outside and the room erupted into squeals, which continued for at least a minute.

"Quiet, everyone, shush," Alice-Miranda commanded, trying to quell the fuss. "Mrs. Howard will—"

Without warning Jacinta's bedroom door flew open.

"Mrs. Howard will what, young lady?" The house mistress panted. "What a ruckus."

There in the doorway, in an orange chenille bathrobe with a floral shower cap perched atop her head, stood Mrs. Howard. Her gaze moved from one girl to the next until it came to rest on Jacinta.

"Jacinta Headlington-Bear, was this *your* idea?"

Jacinta gulped, looked up and nodded slowly.

"Well, tomorrow we'll talk about what you can do to make it up to me. I was about to hop into the bath when I heard such a racket that would wake the dead. I've run all the way from the flat upstairs thinking there was a prowler or the like. And it's just you and your silly 'midnight meetings' at nine o'clock. Off to bed, girls, NOW!"

The party began to break up. No one dared to say a word, except Alice-Miranda.

"Mrs. Howard, please don't blame Jacinta. No one made us come, and apparently it's a bit of a tradition to have a meeting on the first night back. Well, except last term, but that doesn't matter. Please don't be cross. I promise we will make it up to you tomorrow. What about we bring you something extra special for your tea? I can ask Mrs. Smith if she can make your favorite. It's apple-cinnamon bun, isn't it? Is that what you'd like?"

Howie did her best to maintain her furrowed brow, but in the end she could barely restrain the smile that was spreading across her face.

"Oh, dear girl, wherever did you come from?" She shook her head. "Now, off to bed quickly. And no more of this, all right?"

The girls nodded in unison and scampered off to their rooms.

Within a very short time, all that could be heard was the sound of Jacinta's snoring, competing with some rather loud snorts from the flat upstairs.

Chapter 4

Alice-Miranda was awake long before Mrs. Howard's clanging bell roused the rest of the house. She was sitting up in bed reading when Millie yawned and rolled over.

"Good morning," Alice-Miranda greeted her friend.

Millie sat up and rubbed her eyes. "I wish it was still vacation," she grumbled.

"Oh, I don't," Alice-Miranda replied. "I mean, I love being at home, but there are so many things going on here, and I can hardly wait to hear about Miss Grimm's plans for the term."

Millie shook her head. "One day, Alice-Miranda,

when you're as old as me, you'll be completely *over school*."

Alice-Miranda giggled. "I can't imagine what it's like to be as ancient as ten. But I don't think I'll ever be over school. I simply love it—and I know you're only teasing me because secretly you love it too."

"Well, just don't tell anyone," Millie said with a smile, "or you'll ruin my reputation."

At the opposite end of the corridor, Mrs. Howard's shrill morning call began. "Rise and shine, girls, rise and shine. Time to get up, time to sparkle. Chop, chop, choppy chop." Her chorus continued along the hallway, punctuated with loud bursts of bell ringing. She stopped outside the girls' door and knocked firmly before entering.

"Good morning, ladies. I trust you slept well after your *late night*." Mrs. Howard placed her bell on Alice-Miranda's desk and set forth retrieving uniforms from the wardrobe.

"Good morning," they replied in unison before Millie yawned loudly.

"Run along now to your showers. You don't want to be late for breakfast," Mrs. Howard instructed.

"No, that's for sure." Alice-Miranda threw back the covers, leapt out of bed and gathered up her toothbrush and towel. "Mrs. Smith's making creamy scrambled eggs with crispy bacon this morning as a welcome-back treat. And I'll ask her for something extra special for your tea this afternoon, Mrs. Howard, to make up for last night."

Mrs. Howard shook her head, picked up her bell and followed the pair into the hall. "Off you go now." She smiled.

The dining room was abuzz with chatter as the students caught up on all the happenings of the holidays. Clattering cutlery was momentarily stilled when Miss Grimm arrived to take up her seat at the head table alongside Miss Reedy and Mr. Plumpton. Although things had changed remarkably in the past term, the girls were still only getting used to seeing their headmistress on a daily basis. This morning, dressed in a stylish pale pink suit and with her hair pulled back into a low ponytail, Miss Grimm looked much younger than her thirty-seven years. On the way through the dining room, she greeted the students and grinned broadly.

"So what do you think Miss Grimm has in store for us this term?" Jacinta asked as she loaded her fork with another mouthful of scrambled eggs.

"I hope it's something fun, like a trip away, or

maybe a school fair or a carnival," Millie replied. "We've never had anything like that since I've been here."

"Maybe it's a horse show. Miss Grimm seemed keen for girls to bring their ponies back to school this term," said Alice-Miranda.

Jacinta pulled a face. "Oh, I hope not. You know I can't stand horses. That wouldn't be any fun at all."

"Well, we've got assembly this morning, so maybe she's going to tell us then," said Millie.

Alice-Miranda changed the subject. "Has Sloane arrived yet?"

Jacinta stared blankly. "Who?"

"Your new roommate. Sloane Sykes?"

"Oh, no. There was no sign of her before I left the house." Jacinta frowned. "She'd better be nice."

"I'm sure she will be," Alice-Miranda assured her friend.

"But what if I don't like her?" Jacinta pushed a stringy piece of bacon around her plate.

"Of course you'll like her," Alice-Miranda said.

"I'm not like you, Alice-Miranda. I just can't *like* everyone. It's not in my nature. And maybe I'm not always the easiest person to get on with either," Jacinta admitted.

"Come on, Jacinta—I haven't seen you throw a

tantrum in, what, at least a month now?" Millie suppressed a giggle.

"Millie," Alice-Miranda chided.

"I have been trying hard to be better." Jacinta looked serious. "I thought I was pretty well behaved over vacation, wasn't I?"

"Of course you were. Stop worrying, Jacinta," Alice-Miranda soothed. "I'm sure Sloane's lovely, and I'm positive you'll be great friends in no time."

But Jacinta was not yet convinced. "You'd better be right."

The girls finished breakfast, cleared their plates and charged outside into the crisp morning air. Charles Weatherly, the school's head gardener, was tending to the newly planted roses in the quadrangle.

"Hello, Mr. Charles." Alice-Miranda ran and gave him an unexpected hug.

"Well, hello to you too, my girl." Charlie's cornflower-blue eyes twinkled. "It's been rather quiet around here these past two weeks."

"I can see you've been busy. The garden looks lovely," Alice-Miranda replied. "Mr. Greening sends his regards."

Charlie nodded. "He's a good fellow. I'd best be off,

lass. Mrs. Derby's after some roses for Miss Grimm's study. These are just about perfect."

"Yes, they're lovely." Alice-Miranda nodded at the bunch of iceberg blooms in Charlie's hand. Just at that moment she remembered that she had promised to organize that special treat for Mrs. Howard's afternoon tea. Alice-Miranda ran back to Millie and Jacinta and informed them that she was going to see Mrs. Smith before the bell.

"Oh, drat." Millie scowled. "I've left my pencil case back at the house. I've got English first up after assembly, so I'd better go and get it."

"I'll come with you," said Jacinta. "Anyway, I want to see if my roommate has arrived."

"See you later, then." Alice-Miranda waved goodbye to her friends and strode across the quadrangle to the kitchen door.

"Hello, Mrs. Smith!" Alice-Miranda called as she entered the room. In the cavernous space with its rows of stainless steel counters, Mrs. Smith was checking through the lunch menu. She promptly put the paper down and turned with outstretched arms to give her tiny visitor a warm hug.

"Hello there, young lady. How are you this fine morning?"

"Very well." Alice-Miranda nodded. "Thank you for breakfast. It was delicious."

"My pleasure, dear," Mrs. Smith replied. "Now, to what do I owe this early visit?"

"I'm on a special mission." Alice-Miranda climbed up onto the kitchen stool to sit opposite the cook.

"Oh dear—should I be worried?" Mrs. Smith frowned. "It doesn't involve any spontaneous trips, does it, this plan of yours?"

"No, not at all. It's just that last night the girls on our corridor had a midnight meeting. . . ."

"Midnight! My dear girl, you'll be asleep in your arithmetic." Mrs. Smith scowled.

"Well, except that it wasn't midnight at all. It was only nine o'clock and it's a first night tradition, but then Madeline decided that she would tell us a story about a witch in the woods and the girls got a bit scared, and then a branch scraped against the window and everyone squealed, and Mrs. Howard came running and she was a bit cross, especially with Jacinta, but I asked her not to be because it was all our faults, and then I said that I would ask if you could fix something special for her afternoon tea," Alice-Miranda babbled.

"Slow down, young lady." Mrs. Smith shook her head. "So you've come to see if I might make her an apple-cinnamon bun?"

"However did you know?" Alice-Miranda asked.

"My dear, everyone knows that's Howie's favorite. And it just so happens . . ." Mrs. Smith stood up and walked to the other side of the kitchen, returning with a tea-towel-covered tray. "Ta-da!" She pulled the cloth away to reveal the most magnificent apple-cinnamon bun Alice-Miranda had ever seen.

"Perfect." Alice-Miranda grinned and clapped her hands together.

"Now, what was that you were saying about a witch in the woods?" Mrs. Smith asked.

"Just a silly story, that's all," Alice-Miranda replied. "There's no such thing as witches."

"No, of course not." Mrs. Smith shook her head. She knew Alice-Miranda was right, but Doreen Smith had heard the same story—about a witch in the woods—before. And although she knew better, she wasn't entirely convinced that there wasn't a grain of truth in there somewhere.

"All right, young lady. House mistress pacification seems to be taken care of, so you'd better be off to class," Mrs. Smith instructed.

"Thanks, Mrs. Smith—you're the best!" Alice-Miranda hopped down off her stool and scampered out into the sunshine.

Chapter 5

Meanwhile, Millie and Jacinta had made their way back to Grimthorpe House, where Millie quickly retrieved her missing pencil case.

As they walked down the hallway, a shrill voice coming from inside Jacinta's room caught their attention.

"Look, Sloane, look at this. Isn't that Ambrosia Headlington-Bear? She must be your roommate's mother. Imagine always being in magazines and newspapers. She's like royalty. You'd better make friends with her daughter—you never know what you might get us all invited to."

Millie and Jacinta stood outside. Millie pressed

her ear up against the door while Jacinta leaned down to peer through the keyhole.

"Ooh, and make sure you introduce her to your brother as soon as you can. They might get married."

Jacinta's eyes almost popped out of her head. "Married! What are they talking about?"

"And look at this, Mummy," a young voice added. "All those beautiful dresses, and we're the same size. I'm sure she won't notice if one or two go missing."

"What are they doing in there?" Millie whispered, straining to hear.

"Planning a wedding and raiding my wardrobe, by the sound of it." Jacinta's face was getting redder by the second. "Right, that's it."

Jacinta flung open the door, ready to pounce. Millie almost fell over and just managed to steady herself. Sloane and her mother spun around.

"What are you doing?" Jacinta demanded. "Are you looking through my things?"

Sloane slammed the wardrobe door shut and kicked a dress under the nearest bed.

"No, of course not," the young girl replied. "I'm just moving in."

"You must be Sloane Sykes." Millie marched forward to stand beside Jacinta.

"Yes, and you are?" the girl asked, arching her eye-brows.

"I'm Millie and this is Jacinta. She's your room-mate—the one whose things you were just ferreting through."

"Ahem." The woman cleared her throat.

"And you must be Mrs. Sykes." Millie's lips drew tightly together in a straight line.

"Yes, but you can call me September," the woman replied, crossing her arms over her ample chest and striking what seemed to be a modeling pose.

"Did Mrs. Howard let you in here?" Jacinta asked.

"Yes, she told us to make ourselves at home, and so we were just unpacking, weren't we, darling." Mrs. Sykes pointed at the suitcase still lying closed on the bed.

"Yes, Mummy." Sloane smiled at her mother like a piranha in a goldfish bowl.

September Sykes wore skyscraping gold heels and a metallic blue dress so tight and short she must have been vacuum-packed into it. Her waist-length platinum hair bounced in loose curls, and her makeup appeared to have been applied with the aid of a cake decorator's spatula.

Sloane Sykes, in a crisp new uniform, was shorter, thinner and wore only slightly less makeup, which,

{30}

on an eleven-year-old, was more than a little disturbing.

"And what's *your* surname, Millie?" September smiled, revealing a set of dazzlingly white teeth.

"McLoughlin-McTavish-McNoughton-McGill," Millie replied.

"Oooh, that sounds important," September cooed.

"No, not at all." Millie frowned.

Mrs. Howard appeared in the doorway, with Mrs. Derby, the headmistress's secretary, in tow.

"Millicent and Jacinta, what are you doing back here? You know you're not allowed to return to the house after breakfast," Mrs. Howard chided.

"Sorry, Howie," Millie apologized. "I forgot my pencil case."

"And it was just as well we came back, seeing as you've left these two in here alone going through my things," Jacinta snarled.

"Jacinta Headlington-Bear, mind your manners. That's no way to treat your new roommate." Mrs. Howard spun around to face Sloane and her mother, and then turned back to the girls.

"But it's true." Millie nodded.

Mrs. Howard's eyes widened in disbelief. "You two can apologize, please. NOW!"

Millie and Jacinta scowled. With heads bent

toward the floor they both muttered a halfhearted "Sorry."

"That's not like you at all, Millicent. You, on the other hand, Jacinta—well, I hope we're not heading back to the bad old days," Mrs. Howard tutted. "I'm sure the girls will make it up to you, Sloane."

"Don't fuss, Mrs. Howard." September grinned. "Jacinta and Sloane are bound to become best friends. Or rather, BFFs—isn't that what you girls call them these days?"

Jacinta rolled her eyes.

"Yes, well, her manners had better improve by this afternoon. Now, off you go, you two. Lessons are about to start, and you don't want to be late on your first day. Mrs. Derby will bring Sloane over in a little while, once she's had a chance to get properly settled." Mrs. Howard's forehead wrinkled like pin-tucking on a blouse, and she gave Millie and Jacinta one of her best-ever death stares.

The girls marched off. Not a word was spoken until they reached the safety of the veranda.

"What was that?" Jacinta demanded. "Who is that woman? And that girl—I've never seen anyone her age with makeup like that!"

"Don't worry, Jacinta." Millie put her hand on her friend's shoulder. "I wouldn't want to be in her shoes when Miss Grimm and Miss Reedy spot her. She'll be wiping that mascara off in no time."

"But she's awful, and I don't see why I have to be in the same room as her." A fat tear wobbled in the corner of Jacinta's eye.

"It's all right," Millie replied. "She's probably just nervous about being at boarding school."

Millie couldn't believe their bad luck. Alethea Goldsworthy had left big shoes to fill when it came to being the school bully. But if the few moments that Millie had spent with her were anything to go by, Sloane Sykes, it seemed, had very big feet.

Chapter 6

The whole school was seated in the Great Hall for the first assembly of the term. Millie and Jacinta sped into their seats a moment before the staff processional began, with Miss Grimm at the head of the line. She glided down the aisle, a gratified smile on her face as she led the other teachers behind her.

Mr. Trout's organ accompaniment of the school song rose and fell with the fervor of a crashing symphony. But his improvised flourishes at the end of each verse seemed to cause Miss Grimm's mouth to twitch and her grin to disappear.

Ophelia reached the microphone. "Thank you, Mr.

Trout, for your rather—mmm, how to put it—
extravagant recital. Perhaps you'd like to talk to me
about that later?" She looked up at him in the organ
gallery, arched her left eyebrow, then turned back to
face the students. "Good morning, everyone."

"Good morning, Miss Grimm," the students chorused.

"I'd like to welcome you all back for a new term,
and a very exciting one at that. There are some
birthday announcements from Miss Reedy, and then
I'll tell you about a wonderful project we'll be working on over the coming weeks."

Ophelia Grimm sat down and Miss Reedy read the
names of girls who'd had birthdays over the term
break. They were invited to come up onstage and re-
ceive a garland of flowers hand-picked from the garden, which was placed ceremoniously on each head
by Miss Grimm. This was followed by a rousing ren-
dition of "Happy Birthday." Ashima and Susannah
were joined onstage by the sports teacher, Miss Wall.
Her buttercup-yellow wreath clashed horribly with
her cerise-and-blue velvet tracksuit, but she seemed
to enjoy the attention all the same. The birthday
wreaths had been a long-held school tradition until
Miss Grimm had banned the practice, along with
flowers in general. But things were different now at

Winchesterfield-Downsfordvale, and happily, both the flowers and wreaths were back.

With the celebrations over, Miss Grimm again took to the microphone. "Girls, Miss Reedy has been very busy over the break. She's met with Mr. Harold Lipp, the head of English at Fayle School for Boys on the other side of the village. We've decided that it would be timely for us to join forces for a drama production. I do hope you'll take up this opportunity, and I particularly look forward to the splendid play we'll all be able to enjoy toward the end of term. Miss Reedy has the details about auditions and the like and will also explain exactly what you'll be performing."

A ripple of excitement reverberated around the hall. "That's so exciting. . . . My mummy told me they used to do plays with the Fayle boys when she was here. . . . I hope I get a part. . . . What fun. . . . I wonder what play it is?"

Alice-Miranda leaned forward and tapped Jacinta's shoulder. "You know, I think Lawrence is trying to get Lucas a place at Fayle at the moment."

Jacinta swiveled her head and smiled at her friend. "Well, we have to get parts in that play—then we'll be able to see him more than just on the weekends. If he gets to come, of course."

Lucas Nixon had caused quite a fuss when Alice-Miranda and Jacinta first encountered him. Sent to live with his Aunt Lily and Uncle Heinrich, who managed the farm at Alice-Miranda's home, Highton Hall, he seemed to spend most of his time lashing out at everyone around him. But a lot of things had changed very quickly over the holidays: Lucas's absent father turned out to be none other than the famous movie star Lawrence Ridley, who became engaged to Alice-Miranda's beloved Aunt Charlotte. Jacinta and Lucas couldn't stand one another to begin with, but after a couple of weeks, they realized they had much more in common than they could ever have imagined. Jacinta thought it would be wonderful to see him again.

Miss Reedy stood up and walked to the microphone. "Girls, the play we'll be performing is *Snow White and the Seven Dwarfs*. There are plenty of roles, and I'm looking forward to seeing lots of girls try out. Of course, girls can try for boys' roles and vice versa. It should be loads of fun."

Miss Reedy announced that there would be more details about the play up on the bulletin board before the end of the week. Just as she was explaining that if girls were interested in auditioning for parts, they needed to pick up copies of the script from her office that afternoon, a small commotion erupted at the back of the hall. "Ohhhh, did you hear that, darling? A play! How wonderful."

From her position in the rear seats, Alice-Miranda turned to see what was going on. A tall woman with long blond curls was pointing at the stage and talking rather loudly to a young girl standing beside her, who looked remarkably similar.

"Excuse me, can I help you?" Miss Reedy glanced up from her notes and peered over the top of the spectacles perched on the end of her nose.

"Look, Sloane, look at the headmistress and the teachers up there. Oh, they're so cute—like in Harry Potter or something," the woman giggled. The child ignored her, instead splaying the fingers of her left hand and admiring her scarlet nail polish.

With her perfect view of the hall, Miss Grimm had also become aware of the new arrivals. Endeavoring to make them feel welcome, Ophelia decided to introduce the pair to the whole school.

"It's all right, Miss Reedy." Miss Grimm motioned for the English teacher to take her seat, then moved toward the microphone. "Girls and staff, you may have noticed we have some guests. Not guests, in fact, but new members of the Winchesterfield-Downsfordvale family. Please welcome Mrs. Sykes and her daughter, Sloane."

One hundred pairs of eyes swiveled from Miss Grimm back to the newcomers.

"Hello, everyone. Call me September—Mrs. Sykes sounds so old, and well, I'm not old, am I? This is my daughter, Sloane. She's lovely, isn't she?" September wrapped her arm around the girl's shoulder. "We can't wait to meet you all, can we, Sloane? And Sloane's very clever and a fantastic actress. I just heard you saying something about doing a play? Sloane's had acting lessons since she was two, and she's the best dancer ever. So of course, she should be top of the list for the lead role."

Sloane looked up and smirked.

"Yuck, she's even more revolting than I first thought." Millie buried her head in her hands.

"Yes, and she's my roommate," Jacinta whispered.

"No, not Sloane," Millie replied. "I meant her mother."

"Oh." Jacinta grimaced.

Miss Grimm's welcome was losing its gloss as September continued to babble.

"Would you like to take your seat, Sloane?" Miss Grimm pointed toward the front of the hall, near the older students. "And please see me after the assembly as we'll need to have a chat about your . . . face."

"What about my face?" Sloane asked of no one in particular.

"Makeup," Ashima whispered as Sloane took her seat. "We're not allowed."

Sloane rolled her eyes. "Pathetic."

"And, Mrs. Sykes, if you'd like to stay for the remainder of the assembly, you're welcome to sit in the row there just next to you."

September tottered toward the pew, caught her foot on an uneven flagstone and almost fell into Alice-Miranda's lap.

Alice-Miranda caught hold of Mrs. Sykes's arm.

"Ow!" September grimaced. "That hurt."

"I am sorry. I was just trying to help."

"Well, don't bother next time." September Sykes glared at Alice-Miranda, then smoothed her dress and sat bolt upright in her seat. How she could breathe was anyone's guess.

Alice-Miranda turned toward her and smiled. "Hello, my name's Alice-Miranda Highton-Smith-Kennington-Jones," she whispered, and held out her tiny hand. "And I'm very pleased to meet you."

September Sykes's ears pricked up. "Did you say Highton-Smith-Kennington-Jones?"

"Yes." Alice-Miranda nodded. "Do you know my mummy and daddy?"

"Well, sort of, but I'd looove to get to know them better," September simpered, her pearl-white smile widening. She took Alice-Miranda's dainty hand in hers. "It's very nice to meet you too."

September Sykes could not believe her luck. Today was turning out even better than she had hoped.

Chapter 7

The arrival of Sloane and September Sykes caused quite a stir among the girls and staff. At the conclusion of the assembly, Mrs. Sykes seemed very eager to speak with Sloane's teachers and joined the staff as they left the hall. As she bumped in beside Mr. Plumpton, his red nose took on an even brighter glow, particularly when Mrs. Sykes linked her arm through his. Miss Reedy glowered and bit her lip. She wasn't used to such ostentatious displays.

September Sykes didn't notice Miss Reedy's glares. She was too busy loudly describing her glorious modeling career and explaining that Sloane's father regularly appeared on television, although in what capacity she didn't reveal. Mr. Plumpton coughed awkwardly as September leaned in and whispered that, thanks to her stepmother-in-law making provisions for the children's education, Sloane and her older brother, Septimus, were finally exactly where they belonged, at Winchesterfield-Downsfordvale Academy for Proper Young Ladies and Fayle School for Boys.

With a flutter of her lashes, September released Mr. Plumpton's arm and trotted after Miss Grimm "for a little chat." She was convinced that this was only the start of much bigger things for the Sykes family. In her mind, they'd struggled quite long enough and it was about time she had everything she wanted, including that oversized Prada handbag she'd seen on Ambrosia Headlington-Bear's arm in a magazine photograph. Now that she and her children were mixing in the right circles, she was sure life was about to become a whole lot more interesting.

As for the students of Winchesterfield-Downsfordvale, the girls had hurried off to their first lessons aflame with curiosity about the new girl and her remarkable mother. Amid much chatter and speculation, they seemed to have quite a deal of trouble concentrating on their morning classes.

At half past ten, Alice-Miranda was on her way to meet Millie in the dining room for morning tea when she saw Sloane standing on her own near the entrance to the library.

"Are you lost?" Alice-Miranda smiled. "You're Sloane, aren't you? My name's Alice-Miranda Highton-Smith-Kennington-Jones and I'm very pleased to meet you." She offered her tiny hand.

Sloane looked down at her and glared. "No, I'm not lost. I'm just waiting for, what's her name, Dinka or something."

"Oh, you mean Danika. She's the Head Prefect. I suppose Miss Grimm has asked her to show you around. Are you having a good day?" Alice-Miranda continued, "I just love school. And wait until you see what Mrs. Smith has made for our morning tea."

Sloane stared at Alice-Miranda as if she had been promised a roast pork dinner but was served pickled pigs' trotters instead.

Finally she spoke. "Are you always like this?"

"Like what?" Alice-Miranda's eyes widened.

"So . . . happy and bouncy and *enthusiastic.*" Sloane's monotone voice could barely hide her distaste.

"Oh, yes. I can't imagine a reason not to be happy and bouncy and enthusiastic. Winchesterfield-

Downsfordvale is simply the most splendid school ever, and our teachers are lovely and so clever, and Miss Grimm, well, she's the best headmistress in the whole world."

Sloane slowly shook her head. "Good grief!" she muttered under her breath. "And my mother expects me to be friends with someone like you."

"Oh, yes, I'm sure we'll be friends too." Alice-Miranda smiled.

"You can go now." Sloane flicked her hand. "I'm fine, and you don't want to be late for your tea."

"Oh, all right, I think Danika's coming now anyway." Alice-Miranda looked over Sloane's left shoulder. "See you in a minute."

The younger girl waved and then skipped off in the direction of the dining room. As soon as Alice-Miranda's back was turned, the older girl's tongue shot out like a lizard's. Unlike her mother, Sloane Sykes was not the least bit impressed by her new surroundings or the people who inhabited them.

Chapter 8

"Yum, is that strawberry sponge?" Alice-
Miranda licked her lips as she slid into
her seat beside Millie in the dining room.

"Sure is." Millie pushed a plate of the sticky confec-
tion toward her friend.

"I've just had a lovely chat with Sloane," Alice-
Miranda announced.

"I can't imagine how." Jacinta glowered. "You
didn't see what she and her mother were doing when
we went back to the house before."

"What were they doing?" Alice-Miranda quizzed.

"Going through Jacinta's things," said Millie. "And

getting awfully wound up about Jacinta's mother, for some strange reason."

"Oh." Alice-Miranda rested her fork against the side of her plate. "Well, I'm sure they were just excited about being at school. It's such a great adventure being a boarder."

Millie agreed. "That's what I said, but I have to admit that I have a bad feeling about those two. I think Sloane's trouble with a capital T and her mother is even worse."

Alice-Miranda frowned. "I'm sure they'll be fine. Sometimes it just takes a little while to settle into somewhere new."

Jacinta and Millie smiled at their little friend and shook their heads. She could always be relied upon to think the best of everyone.

The bell rang to signify the end of morning tea, and Alice-Miranda, Millie and Jacinta took their dirty plates and cups to the sideboard.

"Are you going to try out for the play?" Alice-Miranda asked the girls.

"Yes, of course," said Millie.

Jacinta nodded. "I wonder if one of the dwarfs could be a gymnast? And what about you Alice-Miranda? Will you audition?"

"I think so—I'm going to get a script from Miss Reedy after school. I can get copies for both of you as well."

The girls parted company, heading off to their various lessons. Alice-Miranda and Millie decided they would take a walk to the stables at lunchtime to see how Alice-Miranda's pony, Bonaparte, was getting on. Jacinta tried not to wrinkle her nose and said she planned to do some gymnastics training instead.

Alice-Miranda had been thrilled that her parents agreed to let Bony come back to school with her. After all, she had settled in so well, and there was no doubt Bonaparte could do with being ridden more often. Hopefully his new surroundings would keep the little monster out of trouble. At least while he was at school he would stay out of Mr. Greening's prized vegetable patch at Highton Hall.

There was only an hour of class time before lunch. Alice-Miranda had her favorite, English class with Miss Reedy, while Millie was at PE and Jacinta had mathematics. Just after one o'clock, Alice-Miranda and Millie met at the dining room, where they collected some sandwiches to take with them to the stables.

They bounded off across the oval and down the lane, chatting between bites of lunch.

"Hello there, Bonaparte," Alice-Miranda called as she and Millie entered the cool brick stable block.

A loud whinny pierced the air, and Bonaparte spun around and thrust his head over the half door of the stable.

"Are you starving again, you poor man?" Millie fetched a loose carrot from the feed room and held it out to him. "Steady on there, greedy guts," she scolded as Bonaparte almost inhaled her hand along with the carrot.

Alice-Miranda picked up a brush, opened the stall door and walked inside. She began giving the pony a quick rubdown. A young lad pushing a wheelbarrow full of straw entered the building and plodded toward them.

"Hello, miss." The boy put the barrow down and addressed Millie. "Is he yours?" He motioned at Bonaparte's stable, where Alice-Miranda was hidden from view.

"No," Millie replied. "Definitely not."

Alice-Miranda scrambled onto the stall door, her feet dangling in the air as she hoisted herself up with her arms. "He's mine."

"Goodness, miss, you do surprise me," the boy replied.

"Why is that?" Alice-Miranda asked.

"Well, he's a bit of a monster, that one—you take care in there."

"Oh dear, have you been a bad boy already, Bonaparte? I'm sorry if he's given you any trouble. He's really very sweet, but he seems to be a bit set against young lads. Our poor Max at home gets it all the time. Just be firm, that's the trick." Alice-Miranda slid down the door. She emerged from the stable and brushed Bonaparte's gray fuzz from her uniform.

"Hello," she said, holding her hand out to the young man. "My name is Alice-Miranda Highton-Smith-Kennington-Jones, and I'm very pleased to meet you, Mr. . . ."

"It's Wally, Wally Whitstable." The boy reached out slowly and shook her hand.

"And this is Millie," said Alice-Miranda. Millie reached forward and shook his hand too.

"Are you new here, Wally?" Millie asked. She noticed he had the most brilliant emerald-green eyes and a shock of red hair to rival her own.

"Yup, Charlie put me on last week—said that there were lots of ponies coming for the term and he needed some help. I like horses, I really do. I'm hoping to be a strapper if I can. I don't imagine racehorses could be any more difficult than that bloke." Wally motioned his head toward Bonaparte.

"That sounds like fun." Alice-Miranda smiled. "And I am sorry about Bony. I hope in time you might learn to like him a little bit. He's really quite lovable when you get to know him."

"Do you have a pony, miss?" Wally asked Millie.

"Yes, his name's Chudley Chops." Millie shook her head and rolled her eyes. "I know, like the dog food. Everyone thought it was a very funny joke when I decided to call him Chudley, and then Dad added Chops because he thought it was hilarious. Anyway, we just call him Chops for short. He's arriving very early on Saturday morning."

"Well, I'll be pleased to make the acquaintance of old Chudley Chops. Now I'd best get off and finish mucking out, and I think by my watch it must be time for your afternoon lessons." Wally excused himself.

Alice-Miranda nodded. "We'll see you soon, Wally. And you behave yourself, Bonaparte. Stay out of trouble."

Bonaparte whinnied loudly in reply and shook his head up and down as if to agree.

"So, you will be a good boy," Alice-Miranda laughed.

"Yes, and I'll believe that when I see it." Millie grabbed her friend's hand and they charged off to class.

Chapter 9

The rest of the week passed by in a blur. Classes were busy, and most of the girls spent any spare time learning lines in preparation for the upcoming auditions. Alice-Miranda, Jacinta and Millie were each trying out for several different parts, but Sloane informed them that there was only one decent role in the whole thing and there was no doubt it would be hers.

Sloane didn't seem especially keen to make friends with anyone, in spite of her mother's insistence that she and Jacinta would become BFFs. Her attempts at conversation usually involved questions about what the girls' parents did and where they lived and if they had a vacation house or a yacht. Alice-Miranda said that Sloane was probably just nervous and not good at making chitchat, but Millie thought she was a bit on the nosy side.

Jacinta and Sloane had come to an uneasy truce. With no further evidence of Sloane meddling with her things, Jacinta decided she would give her a chance. But it wasn't always easy, especially when she overheard Sloane talking to her mother on the telephone and the whole topic of conversation seemed to be her own mother and what she was reportedly up to that week.

At Friday's afternoon tea, which consisted of the most delicious apple pie, Millie asked around to see who would like to go out on a riding party on Saturday.

"Count me in." Alice-Miranda nodded.

"Me too," Susannah agreed.

"Urgh, me not." Jacinta pulled a face. "I've got training, and you know how I feel about horses—I'd rather file my nails."

The other girls laughed.

"What about you, Sloane? Would you like to come riding?" Alice-Miranda asked.

"Um, yes, of course, but my new horse, Harry, hasn't arrived yet. He should have been here, but Mummy messed up the transport," she said sulkily.

"That's all right. I think there are a couple of spare ponies that Mr. Charles is looking after for someone in the village. I'll ask him if you can ride one of those," Alice-Miranda offered.

Sloane hesitated. "Oh, okay."

"They're pussycats, believe me," said Alice-Miranda. "I rode a gorgeous fellow called Stumps last term because Bonaparte was still at home. He's the sweetest little man."

"A *little* pony? I don't think he'll be good enough for me." Sloane seemed to have regained her confidence.

"Oh, he might be small, but he's fast, especially going uphill." Alice-Miranda smiled.

Sloane gulped. "Well, it's just that I'm used to having a really big proper horse, not some dinky pony. I'm just not sure. . . ."

"Oh, come on, Sloane—if you can handle proper horses, I'm sure you'll have no problems with old Stumps." Millie grinned.

And so it was all arranged. Alice-Miranda and Millie marched off to find Mr. Charles and tell him of their plans. A quick visit to Mrs. Smith ensured there would be a picnic feast fit for a king. She insisted that they should have egg sandwiches and tea and scones with jam and cream. The group would ride as far as Gertrude's Grove, where Wally would deliver their spread in time for lunch.

Chapter 10

Just before ten a.m. on Saturday, Sloane Sykes asked her roommate if she had a spare pair of riding breeches she could borrow. And a shirt and helmet and gloves, if possible, as hers were still at home, along with the elusive new horse that was due to arrive any day now. Although Jacinta hated riding, her mother had insisted that she have a complete outfit, just in case she changed her mind. This time Jacinta found herself handing over her belongings quite happily.

"You know, if you don't like to ride, you should just say so," Jacinta offered.

"It's not that at all." Sloane stood admiring her reflection in the long mirror behind their bedroom door. Certainly the outfit suited her.

"Well, there's no shame in saying what you really think," Jacinta tried again.

"I *love* riding and I'm *very good* at it," Sloane said, almost too emphatically.

"Okay then, have a good time." Jacinta pulled on her tracksuit pants and sat down to lace up her shoes. "I'll see you after training."

Sloane was halfway out the door when she turned back. "Does your mother come and take you out on the weekends?"

Jacinta looked up and frowned. "You're kidding, aren't you? I think *your* mother knows more about where my mother is from week to week. I haven't seen her since Christmas."

"Oh," Sloane mouthed. "So I guess I won't be able to meet her anytime soon. My mother was hoping they could have tea together when she comes to collect me for midterm."

"Well, unless every last one of my mother's friends suddenly wind up in the hospital or worse, I can pretty much guarantee that I'll be staying here for midterm, so tell your mother that if she hoped to meet the oh-so-famous Ambrosia Headlington-Bear, she's going to be sorely disappointed."

Jacinta picked up her gym bag and pushed past Sloane. She was very glad she wasn't going riding. Horses weren't the only thing she found irritating.

Sloane was beginning to wonder what the point of being at boarding school really was. So far, she hadn't met anyone remotely famous, and her roommate's mother was turning out to be a huge disappointment. As for being invited away on holidays, she hadn't any prospects yet. School was okay—the lessons were quite good and the teachers seemed to know their stuff—but what use was it if you didn't get to meet the right people?

Her mother promised that boarding school would change her life. In fact, both Sloane's parents had been thrilled when her stepgranny Henrietta had arranged for her and her brother to go to boarding school. The old woman didn't have any children of her own, so when she married Sloane's grandfather, Percy Sykes, rather late in life, she inherited Sloane and Septimus as grandchildren. When Percy died last year and left Sloane's parents his grocery shop with the flat above, they sold the lot quick smart, even though Henrietta was supposed to be able to live there for as long as it suited her. In September's opinion, Henrietta was both ancient and dotty, so she convinced her husband that the elderly lady would be better served in an aged person's home. It hadn't been too hard for them to shuffle her off to a place called Golden Gates. The nurses told September and Smedley that Henrietta kept asking to see her family. But Henrietta didn't have any other relatives, so clearly, thought September, the old woman *was* losing her mind!

Sloane had started to wonder if her mother thought she was an inconvenience too, just like Granny Henrietta. She glanced at her watch and went to telephone her mother. September insisted that she call home every day for an update.

"Hello, Mummy." Sloane sounded less than excited.

"Well, how are you getting on, then? Where have you been invited to?" her mother asked.

"Nowhere. It's completely dull here and I want to come home," Sloane nagged. "The girls are all so boring, and they don't do anything fun. Jacinta told me her mother won't even be coming to get her at midterm."

"Well," said September, changing tack, "try someone else, then. You know the little one's parents are completely loaded. I think you'll find they're richer than the Queen—and most likely related."

"Good grief, no. She's the most painful Pollyanna

I've ever met. She smiles *all* the time and she's happy *all* the time and she never complains about anything, not ever. It's just not normal," Sloane grouched. "And when are you sending my horse? I'm going riding today and I have to borrow this horrid little pony—and I had to sponge Jacinta's riding gear as well. If you want me to fit in here, I can't be borrowing things all the time."

"Sloane, you know we can't afford a horse," her mother whispered. "What with your grandfather only leaving us such a dreadful, cheap little shop and flat. But don't worry; your father's new business is going to be a license to print money. It won't be long until we can buy you everything you could possibly want. But for now, you know there's no harm in borrowing. If the girls offer, it would be rude not to."

Sloane hung up the phone. In her opinion, life simply wasn't fair.

Chapter 11

Millie, Alice-Miranda and Susannah were already in the stables when Sloane appeared. She looked the part in her borrowed gear, and the girls all commented on her beautiful riding jacket. Sloane didn't tell them it was actually Jacinta's— she couldn't see the point.

Wally Whitstable had been busy helping the girls saddle their mounts. Bonaparte was now standing beside Chops, flicking the older pony with his tail. They'd already had a mighty squabble that had ended with Bonaparte giving Chops a nasty nip on the neck.

"He seems to be in a bit of a mood, miss." Wally

gave Bonaparte a friendly pat on the backside and was nearly kicked for his trouble.

"I don't know what's gotten into him." Alice-Miranda shook her head. She looked her pony in the eye. "Bonaparte Napoleon Highton-Smith-Kennington-Jones, you stop that behavior at once or there will be no treats and no ride."

At the mention of treats, Bony whinnied loudly.

"No, I said, *no treats*—you need to understand the difference," Alice-Miranda tutted.

"Hurry up, Sloane," Millie directed. "That's Stumps in there. You'll need to put his bridle on."

Sloane entered the stall. Stumps was already saddled, with his lead rope tied loosely to a hook on the wall. There was a bridle hanging on the back of the stall door. Sloane grabbed it and tried to work out what went where.

"Okay, let's put this on," she muttered under her breath. Sloane approached the pony and began to force the bridle over his head. Unfortunately she hadn't yet undone the straps and it was proving more than a little difficult.

Wally had just finished helping Susannah with her pony Buttercup, when he spotted Sloane.

"Would you like some help there, miss?" he asked.

"Yes, you should have done it already." Sloane let

go of the bridle and it fell to the ground. "I haven't got time to be fussing around with that silly thing."

"Well, if you want to go riding, then I think *that silly thing* is rather important." Wally retrieved the bridle from the floor and undid the throat lash. "Would you like to give me a hand?"

"No, not especially. Isn't that what *you* get paid for?" Sloane sneered at the lad.

Alice-Miranda walked over to Stumps's stable. "If you're nervous, Sloane, that's perfectly all right. My daddy says that it's good to be wary around horses no matter how well you know them. Bonaparte always keeps me on my toes."

"I'm not nervous. Don't be ridiculous. It's just that stupid silver thing—it's not the same as the one I have at home." Sloane pouted.

Millie and Susannah joined them.

"You mean the bit, is that what you're talking about?" Millie's suspicions that Sloane wasn't a rider were beginning to ring true.

"Yes, of course I meant the bit—what else would I be talking about?" Sloane's eyes drilled into Millie.

Wally finished bridling Stumps and led the pony out into the passageway. "Well, he's all yours, miss." He handed the reins to Sloane.

"This is going to be such fun." Alice-Miranda pulled

a stool up beside Bonaparte and nimbly hopped onto his back with the expertise of someone who had been riding most of her life. Millie didn't bother with the stool and easily hauled herself onto Chops's back. Susannah's much larger horse, Buttercup, swayed lazily as she put her foot into the stirrup and swung gently into the saddle. This left Sloane marooned beside Stumps.

"Would you like a leg up, miss?" Wally offered.

Sloane shook her head and pulled a stool up next to the pony.

"Excuse me, miss," Wally began. "You're not going to get on from there are you?"

"Why?" Sloane looked around. The other girls were sitting atop their mounts waiting for her.

"Because that's the far side of the horse and you never get on that side. Usually scares them."

Sloane gulped loudly. "Well, at my riding school, we always get on from this side. My riding teacher went to the Olympics and he rode the Spanish dancing horses too."

"Gosh, that's amazing!" Alice-Miranda gasped.

"Weird, more like it," Millie added. "I've never heard of anyone who's been in the Olympics *and* with the Spanish dancing horses."

"Well, it's true," Sloane snapped. "And if you don't believe me, I won't bother coming."

"Of course we believe you, Sloane," Alice-Miranda soothed. But Alice-Miranda had a strange feeling that something wasn't quite right—and if there was one thing she was usually right about, it was her strange feelings.

Stumps began to snort. As Sloane attempted to throw her leg over his back, he spun around and butted her bottom with his head. She fell to the ground with a thud, right in the middle of a freshly steaming pile of manure deposited moments ago by Bonaparte.

"Ahh!" she cried. "You little beast. Look at me!"

Sloane's white riding breeches now resembled the patchy hide of a Guernsey cow.

"There, there, miss." Wally grabbed the pony's reins and wheeled him back around. "I think the poor fellow just got a bit nervous. Perhaps if you try getting on the usual way? An old bloke like Stumps is not used to fancy Spanish riding habits."

Sloane picked herself off the floor. She was sorely tempted to tell the other girls she wasn't feeling well.

"Are you all right, Sloane?" Millie asked. "You know, you don't have to come if you don't want to."

But Sloane took Millie's comment as a challenge and she was determined to prove the little brat wrong.

"I'm fine," she spat, and this time, standing on the near side of the pony, she swung herself into the saddle. Stumps stood perfectly still—not even an ear twitched.

"Well, come on then, everyone, let's go!" Alice-Miranda clicked her tongue and the group moved off into the bright sunshine.

Chapter 12

Millie and Chops led the group as they made their way down the lane into the woods. Sloane spent most of the time watching how the other girls managed their ponies. She'd been on a horse only once before, at the local show on a lead rope. But no one needed to know that now, and besides, she seemed to be doing quite well.

The group walked and then trotted for a while. When Millie called out that they were going to canter, Sloane yelled back that she thought Stumps was tired and they could go on without her if they wanted.

"Of course we won't race off." Alice-Miranda slowed down and rode alongside her.

Millie rolled her eyes. She was bursting to take Chops for a proper gallop. As if reading her mind, Alice-Miranda suggested that Millie and Susannah have a race to Gertrude's Grove. She and Sloane would meet them there in a little while.

Millie didn't need any more encouragement.

"Thanks, Alice-Miranda," she called. "See you there!"

Chops and Buttercup hit their strides within seconds, leaving Alice-Miranda and Sloane doddling along together.

"Bonaparte's tired too." Alice-Miranda smiled. "Do you have any brothers or sisters, Sloane?"

"I have a stinky brother who's a year older than me," she replied.

"That's lovely." Alice-Miranda nodded. "Not that he's stinky, but that you have a brother. I'd love to have a brother or sister, but Mummy says that it wasn't to be. So there's just me and Mummy and Daddy at home. Oh, and Mrs. Oliver and Shilly, and Max and Cyril and the Greenings and Lily and Heinrich and Jasper and Poppy and Daisy and, of course, Granny Bert."

"Do they *all* live with you?" Sloane asked in astonishment.

"Oh, no, not at all. Daisy and Granny live at Rose

Cottage and the Bauers live down the lane and the Greenings live in the gatehouse. Max and Cyril have a flat over the stables, so only Mrs. Oliver and Shilly live in the Hall with Mummy and Daddy and me."

"Where do you live?" Sloane asked.

"Near a lovely little village called Highton Mill. It's terribly pretty. Our house is called Highton Hall," Alice-Miranda replied.

"Is it very big?" Sloane continued.

"It's certainly not as big as some of our friends' houses, but there's plenty of room. Tell me about your brother. What's his name?"

"Septimus." Sloane smirked. "He's foul."

"I'm sure he can't be that bad." Alice-Miranda smiled. "Does he go to school close by?"

"He's at Fayle," Sloane replied, then giggled. "He'll probably fail at Fayle."

"I don't think so," Alice-Miranda said. "It's against the school charter. It's such a funny name for a school, isn't it? I asked Miss Reedy however it came to be called that and she told me that the man who started the school was Mr. Frederick Erasmus Fayle and he wrote a strict charter, which is sort of like a set of rules, I think, about the importance of academic standards. Do you know, the school motto is *'Nomine defectus non autem natura,'* which means

'Fail by name, not by nature.' That's terribly clever, don't you think? If more than twenty-five percent of boys fail any test, the school has to close immediately, and whoever is next in line in the Fayle family can do with it whatever they choose. Wouldn't that be a terrible shame? A grand school like that closed down. Mr. Fayle must have been a very proud man to make that rule. Anyway, Millie, Jacinta and I have a friend who we hope might be starting there soon. His name's Lucas, and his father is going to marry my Aunt Charlotte. Maybe he and your brother will become friends?"

"Whatever." Sloane stared off into the distance. "Do you think we could trot for a while? I'm hungry."

"Of course." Alice-Miranda clicked her tongue and Bonaparte picked up the pace. She rose and fell with the trot. Sloane just bounced along on top of Stumps.

When the girls finally reached Gertrude's Grove, Wally had already met Millie and Susannah with a basket and picnic blanket and driven away again. Sloane threw her right leg forward over Stumps's neck and slid off the pony, hitting the ground with a thud.

"That was a fancy dismount," Alice-Miranda said admiringly. Sloane raised her nose in the air and did her best attempt at stalking off toward the picnic.

Trouble was, she could barely stand, let alone walk gracefully.

"Do you want some help with Stumps?" Alice-Miranda offered.

"Yes, you can tie him up for me, can't you?" Sloane didn't even look back. Alice-Miranda grabbed Stumps's reins and looped them over the nearby gate. She made sure Bonaparte was far enough away that he couldn't get up to any mischief. It was never a good idea to tether him within reach of another pony.

"You took your time," Millie called as she looked up from where she was rummaging through the wicker basket. "We've been here for ages, but Wally just arrived with the food a few minutes ago."

"There's a lovely stream over there beyond the willows," Susannah added. "We had a competition skimming stones."

"And I won." Millie smiled.

Sloane hobbled over and gingerly lowered herself down onto the edge of the picnic blanket. Her grimace said it all.

"Sore backside, hey?" Millie queried. "Usually happens when you haven't been on a horse for a while."

"I'm fine," Sloane retorted. "And who said I hadn't been on a horse for a while?"

"Well, it's dead obvious—" Millie began.

"And what's that supposed to mean?" Sloane snapped, a crimson rash rising up her neck.

Alice-Miranda arrived just in time to survey the delicious-looking spread that would be their lunch. "Ohh, look at that!" she gasped, interrupting Millie and Sloane's exchange.

Susannah had unwrapped a stack of sandwiches; there was egg and lettuce, ham, cheese and tomato, turkey, Brie and cranberry, not to mention roast beef with a touch of horseradish. From the bottom of the basket, Susannah retrieved four plump scones, a pot of jam and another of cream, and four large slices of devil's food cake. There were two thermoses, one filled with tea and the other with hot chocolate.

Sloane reached forward and helped herself to a slice of cake.

"Would you like to have a sandwich first?" Alice-Miranda offered.

"No, I hate sandwiches. Unless they're fully organic, and I can't tell, so I'd rather not have any," Sloane replied.

Millie raised her eyebrows. "But it's all right to have a huge piece of chocolate cake?"

"What's it to you?" Sloane bit into the cake.

It seemed that the school's newest student didn't have the easiest nature, but Alice-Miranda was determined to make her feel part of the group, and hurriedly changed the subject.

"You know, I came through here when I was on my hike last term," she commented. "And then I headed over the stream and up into the mountains. It was so lovely."

"I still can't believe you had to do it." Susannah smiled. "I would have been so scared."

"Well, I was a little bit nervous, but I knew that there was nothing out here to hurt me," said Alice-Miranda.

"Except the witch," Susannah lowered her voice and widened her eyes.

"A witch. As if!" Sloane scoffed. "You're such a baby. I'm not going hiking. Ever!"

"Miss Grimm will have something to say about that," Millie replied.

"Really? I don't think so. Mummy says hikes are for tomboys, and I'm hardly that, am I, now?" Sloane spat.

"Would you like something else to eat, Millie?" Alice-Miranda hurriedly handed her friend a jam-smothered scone.

"Thanks." Millie rolled her eyes at Sloane, who fortunately was looking elsewhere.

The scrumptious lunch had a soothing effect and the girls had a lovely time eating and lying about in the warm sunshine. The ponies were behaving themselves too, with barely a snort or grunt out of any of them. Amid the chirping of birds, the only other sound was the tearing of clumps of grass as Bony and his friends enjoyed the sweet tastes of the meadow.

"I'm so full!" Millie patted her stomach and lay back with her head in Alice-Miranda's lap.

"Me too," wailed Susannah.

The girls had all but demolished Mrs. Smith's feast, leaving only a couple of half-sandwiches and one lonely scone.

"Look." Alice-Miranda pointed at the gate. "There's Wally."

The clattering of the old school Land Rover filled the air and Wally Whitstable pulled up beside them. The engine shuddered to a halt and he hopped out of the vehicle.

Wally eyed the remains of the picnic. "Goodness, you lot must have been famished."

"Yes, but now we're all as full as ticks." Alice-Miranda sighed.

"Not me." Sloane turned up her nose. "Some of us watch how much we eat."

Millie sat up and offered Wally a leftover sandwich.

"Thanks, miss," he said. "I'm a bit hungry myself. It's been a busy morning. I've been giving some riding lessons to a couple of the girls who aren't very confident. Perhaps you'd like to join them next time, Miss Sloane?"

"Why?" snapped Sloane. "I don't need lessons with beginners."

"Well, the offer's there." Wally wolfed down the roast beef sandwich.

Alice-Miranda and Susannah set to, packing the thermoses and other bits and pieces into the picnic basket. Millie picked up the blanket and tried to fold it, but she couldn't quite get the two ends lined up. Sloane ignored her.

Millie let out a shuddering sigh. "Do you think you could give me hand?"

"Oh, all right," Sloane replied, grabbing at the other end of the blanket. Anyone would have thought she'd been asked to scrub a toilet with a toothbrush.

"Here, Miss Millie, I'll do that," Wally said.

"It's all right, Wally. Sloane's helping me," said Millie with narrowed eyes.

{75}

"Then let me carry that basket to the car," he offered as Alice-Miranda and Susannah struggled with the enormous wicker hamper.

When the blanket was finally folded and stowed in the four-wheel drive, Wally said, "I'd best be off, girls. Are you heading straight back?"

"Yes, I think so," Millie replied. "We need to learn our lines for the auditions next week."

"Well, be careful." Wally hopped into the driver's seat. "Oh, and by the way, Miss Sloane, just watch Stumps—I've heard he can be a bit of a bolter on the inbound run, but I'm sure an experienced rider like you won't have any trouble with him. Just don't mention the 'h' word." Wally winked at Millie, who smothered a smile.

"What do you mean, the 'h' word?" Sloane called out over the clattering engine of the four-wheel drive. But Wally was halfway up the hill.

"You just have to make sure you keep a tight rein on him, that's all," said Alice-Miranda. "Don't worry. I'll ride with you the whole way. If the other girls want to race, that's fine. I won't leave you."

Susannah and Millie walked off to get Chops and Buttercup from where they were tied up farther down the fence line. Alice-Miranda hauled herself up onto Bonaparte and watched as Sloane attempted three times to get onto Stumps. Thankfully, he really was a dozy old fellow and didn't even flinch when, on the fourth attempt, she landed a thumping blow to the side of his ribs with her right boot. Alice-Miranda wasn't concerned about Stumps's alleged habit of bolting for home. Whenever she'd ridden him last term, he'd been the gentlest chap she'd ever met.

Millie and Susannah joined Alice-Miranda and Sloane. The four of them were standing abreast when Sloane leaned forward and asked, "Well, are we heading straight *home* or what?"

With the mere mention of the word, Stumps let out an ear-piercing whinny. He threw his head back and forth, pawed at the ground and then took off, from zero to gallop in barely a second.

"Ahhhhhhhhhhhhhh!" Sloane screamed as she leaned forward and clutched Stumps's shaggy mane. Millie, Alice-Miranda and Susannah knew they had to catch up—and fast.

"Hold on, Sloane, we're coming!" Alice-Miranda called as she dug her heels into Bony's sides and urged him after the runaway horse.

Stumps flew across the open meadow, through the stream and toward the woods. Sloane continued screeching as the girls raced to catch up. Millie and

Chops were the fastest—his little legs pumped as Millie sat glued to the saddle.

As they neared the woods, Susannah yelled, "Keep your head down, Sloane!"

Sloane ducked just in time as a branch grazed the top of her riding helmet. The ponies were flying through the undergrowth, snorting and puffing.

Up ahead, Sloane could just make out the shape of a fallen tree. She realized that Stumps was not about to stop and braced herself as the pony flew through the air and cleared the trunk with no trouble. Surprisingly, she was still on his back when he landed. Millie and Chops easily managed the jump with Susannah and Alice-Miranda close behind. The ponies raced on. Stumps was increasing his lead. Who would have thought the old boy had it in him?

The woodland gave way to a clearer path, lined on either side by thick undergrowth. Sloane's screams echoed through the forest. The trail narrowed and then, without warning, split into two paths. Sloane and Stumps were nowhere to be seen. Chops and Buttercup headed left, and despite Alice-Miranda's best efforts to follow them, Bonaparte veered to the right. Alice-Miranda jerked the reins as hard as she could. She ordered Bony to stop, but a small child of seven and a half is no match for a pony on a mission.

As Chops and Buttercup thundered on in the other direction, with Sloane's shrieks fading in the distance, Alice-Miranda was aware of Bonaparte sniffing the air around him. In spite of his pace, he was lifting his head and inhaling wildly. Alice-Miranda knew this could only mean one thing—cabbages!

Chapter 13

Alice-Miranda and Bonaparte thundered on through the woods until Bonaparte finally came to a halt outside what must once have been a gigantic vegetable patch. Bounded by a tumbledown fence still high enough to keep the pony out, Alice-Miranda had just managed to stop herself from flying over his head when Bony stopped dead in his tracks. She could see the overgrown rows of gardens, a jumble of weeds sprouting from the hardened earth—rather like Mr. Trout's uncontrollable clumps of ear hairs, she thought.

"It's about time you stopped, Bonaparte Napoleon

Highton-Smith-Kennington-Jones," Alice-Miranda panted. "Thank goodness for that fence. You're a very naughty pony. And there are no cabbages here anyway, you silly old boy. I don't know where we are or how far we've come. And poor Sloane—I hope she's all right."

Bonaparte whinnied and pawed at the ground, eager to see for himself whether there was anything worth having in the patch. But Alice-Miranda had had enough. She was a very good rider, although no child her age could match Bony's strength when he decided there were free vegetables on offer.

Alice-Miranda looked about her. She had been so preoccupied with getting Bonaparte to stop, she hadn't really taken much notice of where they were. But she did recall passing through a set of enormous derelict gateposts. As Alice-Miranda wheeled Bonaparte around, she noticed a large outbuilding in the distance. She decided to see if there was anyone who might be able to help her find her way back to school.

Digging her heels in, Alice-Miranda urged Bonaparte forward. But he stayed put. She tried again, giving him a sharp kick to the left flank, but he refused to move. There was only one thing for it. She felt in her jacket pocket and found five slightly crumbled sugar cubes. Alice-Miranda dismounted and pulled the reins over Bonaparte's head, then showed the greedy pony one cube. He whinnied loudly and reached out to snaffle the treat from her outstretched hand.

"I have some more, Bony," Alice-Miranda informed him. "But only if you follow me."

Bonaparte might have been stubborn, but he was not stupid. He decided that it was better to have *some* treats than none. He followed Alice-Miranda back toward the outbuilding. She stopped every twenty paces and offered the little beast another cube, which he greedily gulped.

Along the gravel pathway, ancient urns on tall plinths poked through the undergrowth. Alice-Miranda thought they looked quite like some she had at home at Highton Hall, except for their state of decay.

As the tiny girl and her pony reached the building, she realized that there were, in fact, several separate structures bounded by a high brick wall. The entrance to the complex was through a magnificent stone archway, now flecked with mold and decay. Alice-Miranda imagined that in the past it had seen the coming and going of many a splendid carriage. In the forecourt there was a small yard, which she decided would be a perfect pen for Bony while she had a look around.

The main structure had been a very handsome stable block but was now in tumbledown disrepair. The slate roof looked like a patchwork quilt, and the timber doors were missing several panels.

Alice-Miranda coaxed Bonaparte over the cobblestones and into the enclosure and handed over the last sweet reward.

"Now you stay here." She glared at Bony. "And don't you get any thoughts about going back to that patch."

Alice-Miranda checked twice that the rusted chain was secure. Just as she was about to head inside the main building, a large tabby cat appeared and started rubbing against her leg, purring loudly. She turned around to check on Bony and noticed that three more cats, in shades of ginger, gray and black, were now taking up various positions around the yard. One on a windowsill, another atop the wall that enclosed the stable block, and the other had bravely sidled up to Bonaparte, who was now engaged in a sniff-off with the black intruder.

"What a lot of cats," Alice-Miranda said to herself. "You be nice to that kitty, Bonaparte," she warned. "He's probably got a good old set of claws on him."

Alice-Miranda left the yard and entered the stable

block. Immediately her nostrils were assaulted by the smell of damp hay and horses.

"Hellooo," she called. "Is there anyone here?"

The musty brick building creaked and groaned as if apologizing for its current state. She soon realized that there were no animals inside any of the stalls, but the open booth at the end of the passageway was full of ancient saddles and bridles, their leather split and dry, brass fittings tarnished and bits blackened with the passing of time. Several pairs of long riding boots were lined up on a shelf alongside a selection of moth-eaten velvet hats and helmets all coated in thick dusty webs. It didn't look like anyone had been in the tack room for a very long time.

In what would have been the feed room, a row of timber hoppers stood open, their contents of oats and barley long gone. A few loose remnants of straw littered the floor and a large open vat of molasses contained an array of grasshoppers and bugs, fossilized in their amber trap.

"Helloooooo?" Alice-Miranda's voice echoed through the rafters. She wondered if there might be a flat above the stables just like they had at home. But she couldn't see a staircase. Her voice brought no human reply, but the yowling of several cats filled the air.

Alice-Miranda decided that a stable block such as

this would no doubt belong to a large house. She wanted to keep exploring but her watch said that it was now half past two. Millie, Susannah and Sloane should have been home by now. Perhaps they would come looking for her.

Emerging into the afternoon sunshine, Alice-Miranda shielded her eyes and waited for them to adjust to the light. Bonaparte acknowledged her presence with a snort. He was dozing against the gate with one eye open, watching the black cat, who had now taken up residence on top of the feed bin which hung over the gate.

"All right, Bony, there's no one here. But I see you've got plenty of friends to keep you company, so I'm off to find the house that must belong to these stables." Alice-Miranda patted the top of another ginger cat's head as it rubbed its neck up and down her riding boot.

The estate was dotted with handsome trees, claret ash, oak and fir, many of which Alice-Miranda recognized from her outings with her own gardener at home, Mr. Greening. He loved that she asked him so many questions about the names of the plants, and although she was still only seven and a half, Alice-Miranda's knowledge of botanical species was something Mr. Greening was secretly very proud of.

As she walked farther along the driveway, the grassy edges were replaced with a cobblestoned guttering, a sure indication that somewhere up ahead there would be a house. No one would go to that much trouble for a road to nowhere, Alice-Miranda was certain. Through the jungle of branches, she spied an overgrown lawn. A huge ornate fountain sat partially hidden by the mass of weeds and waist-high grass.

"Hellooooo," she called again. The only reply was the meow of a cat. Alice-Miranda looked down to see that the tabby from the stables had joined her on her walk. "Oh, hello, puss." She reached down and patted the top of his head. "Fancied an outing, did you?"

All of a sudden, Alice-Miranda had a strange feeling that she was being watched. She turned around to see that her tabby friend had been joined by at least ten more cats padding along silently behind her.

"Goodness me, there are an awful lot of you indeed," she addressed her feline audience. "Do you *all* live here?"

An uneasy recollection invaded her mind. "Cats, lots of cats," she said aloud, before dismissing the thought. Alice-Miranda didn't believe in witches. They were only in fairy stories.

Chapter 14

Like the Pied Piper with his merry followers, Alice-Miranda continued her way up the drive. She rounded a sweeping bend, where the foliage was so thick it created an arch like a giant's rib cage from one side of the road to the other. Another set of iron gates, hanging open from their limestone columns, beckoned her to enter. There was a name on the left-hand pillar, obscured by a tangle of ivy stuck fast to the tarnished brass plate. She reached up as high as she could and tried to pull back the greenery. It was tricky, but Alice-Miranda caught a handful of leaves and wrenched hard. She traced the blackened outline of the words *Caledonia Manor*.

Alice-Miranda knew the house couldn't be too far away. She began to jog, anxious to find out if there was anyone at home who could set her in the right direction. Her furry friends circled around her, some racing in front as if they knew exactly where to go. Up ahead, she could have sworn she saw a black figure scurrying into the bushes.

"Hellooooooo," Alice-Miranda called. "Can you help me, please? I seem to be lost." But the figure disappeared and so Alice-Miranda continued on her way.

At last, the trees thinned out and there it was in front of her. "Goodness." She drew in a sharp breath. "What an amazing house."

Caledonia Manor was indeed an amazing house. Its ancient limestone blocks glinted in the sunshine. Four Ionic columns formed a magnificent portico with five steps leading to the most enormous double entrance doors Alice-Miranda had ever seen. Her own house, Highton Hall, was renowned as one of the most beautiful homes in the country, but surely Caledonia Manor could once have been included in the same company.

On closer inspection, Alice-Miranda could see that the manor was at the mercy of silent invaders. Tendrils of Virginia creeper grew across some of the upstairs window frames, and grass as tall as Alice-Miranda peered through the downstairs casements. Alice-Miranda could not even see the whole house, so dense were the bushes at the far end. But she could smell smoke, and that had to be a good thing. It meant there was a fire in a hearth somewhere close by.

She marched up the front steps and pressed the discolored brass buzzer beside the door. Then she listened for any sound from within. Nothing. Alice-Miranda clasped the lion's head knocker in the center of the door with both hands and attempted to loosen it from the grip of time. But it was rusted in place and the door was firmly locked.

She looked around to see that her feline followers had disappeared, except for one last tabby, who she spied heading around the corner of the building. Surely the cats would know best where to find the house's owner? After all, they were a well-fed-looking bunch, and that couldn't just be the result of mousing in the stables.

The windows were thick with grime, giving no opportunity at all to see inside. As she beat a path around the side and came to the back of the building, she realized that the house was a vast

U-shape, with an open terrace at the rear. The land behind the manor was far less densely vegetated than at the front. There was evidence of an expansive lawn stepping down from one level to the next, with rows of stone balustrade still zigzagging across its width.

It was only now, when she could take in the whole building, that Alice-Miranda noticed the entire roof of the wing opposite was missing. Blackened rafters poked from the top, and the long wall bore holes like Swiss cheese where once there had been windows.

Alice-Miranda scampered to the top of the terrace and saw her furry friends milling about together at the end of the veranda.

"Hellooooo," she called as the cats meowed, rubbed against each other and wound themselves in and out of her legs. "Is anyone home?"

Alice-Miranda moved toward what looked like the kitchen door. There was still no sign of anyone, but when she tried the door handle this time, it opened. Without a second's hesitation, Alice-Miranda marched inside. Indeed she was right. A large fuel stove dominated the room. The old-fashioned iron cooker sat beside an open fireplace, where a small bundle of kindling was well alight. There was a huge double

Butler's sink and taps that looked like they had come straight from a museum. Saucepans hung on treacherous-looking hooks above the fireplace, and a kettle boiled on the stovetop. Someone was home, somewhere.

Chapter 15

Sloane's knees stopped trembling for the first time since she was unceremoniously dumped by Stumps in yet another pile of manure. Her face, as pale as parchment, was beginning to regain some color as she sat on a straw bale, moaning softly to herself.

"Are you feeling any better?" Susannah asked, patting Sloane on the shoulder.

"Don't touch me!" Sloane spat. "My legs hurt, my backside hurts and I think I might die."

"Well, Miss Sloane, I did try to warn you not to mention the 'h' word," said Wally Whitstable as he handed her a cup of hot cocoa.

"How was I to know what you meant?" Sloane sniffed.

Millie spun around to face her. "Well, if you're half the rider you say you are, you'd know exactly what that meant."

"At my riding school, we don't know about that, because our horses aren't ill-tempered enough to do what that little brute did." Sloane slurped her drink and cast a death stare toward Stumps's stable.

Millie glanced at her watch. "Alice-Miranda should be here by now. I thought she was right behind you, Susannah."

Susannah frowned. "I thought she was too, but then, do you remember that fork in the road? I wonder if she might have gone the other way."

"She wouldn't have done it on purpose," said Millie. She was starting to worry. Although she knew Alice-Miranda to be a very capable rider, she was also aware that Bonaparte could be a little monster. "Wally, do you think I should go and look for her?"

"Let's give her a few more minutes," he replied.

Charlie appeared at the stable door. "Let's give who a few more minutes?" he asked.

"Alice-Miranda," Millie said. "We rode out to Gertrude's Grove this morning, but on the way back Sloane said the 'h' word and Stumps bolted. We were all chasing after her, but then Alice-Miranda disappeared. She should have been back by now."

"Yes, she said that she would ride back with me the whole way, the little liar." Sloane pouted.

"Oh, do be quiet, Sloane. Just because you're the most pathetic rider I've ever seen! Consider yourself lucky not to be in the hospital." Millie stood with her hands on her hips.

"Now, now, Miss Millie, that's not like you," Charlie chastised. "Don't worry about the little one. We'll give her another ten minutes and then we can take the Land Rover out and have a look. You know she's smart. Bonaparte's probably thrown a shoe and she's walking him back so he doesn't go lame."

"Yes, that's probably it." Millie nodded, glad that Charlie had thought of such a sensible explanation. But Millie had a niggling feeling about Alice-Miranda being out there in the woods on her own. Even though it was still only midafternoon, the sooner Alice-Miranda was back home safely, the better, as far as Millie was concerned.

Chapter 16

A lice-Miranda called out three times before she decided she'd have to venture farther inside Caledonia Manor in order to find its occupants.

She exited the kitchen through a door which led to a long passageway. At the end, the ceiling opened up double height to a stately entrance hall dominated by an elegant carved staircase. It was truly a magnificent piece of craftsmanship, rising in one broad flight before splaying left and right to an enormous gallery landing above. Most of the furniture in the hall was hidden under yellowed sheets, while a thick lashing of dust covered the flagstone floor. Alice-Miranda noticed that the only footsteps unsettling the grime were her own, so she decided that whoever lived in the house did not use that route to get to the second floor. She returned to the kitchen, thinking she might find a set of back stairs like the ones at home.

Alice-Miranda tried another door off to the left. She turned the handle and was surprised to find it locked.

"Hello?" she called. "Is anyone in there? I need some help, please. You see, I'm lost and I don't know how to find my way back to school."

There was no reply.

She tried another door opposite. The handle turned. Alice-Miranda opened it to find that the passage led to a smaller hallway with a much plainer staircase.

"Helloooo, is anyone up here?" she called as she climbed, every step creaking more noisily than the one before. At the top of the stairs, Alice-Miranda could see that she was at the far end of the landing she had spied from the front hall. She was about to explore further when there was a loud crash downstairs. Alice-Miranda ran as quickly as she could down the back stairs and into the kitchen, where she glimpsed a flash of black scurrying through the door which had previously been locked.

"Stop!" she called. "Please, come out. I'm lost and

I'd really like to talk to you." She heard the door click shut. And then she saw it: a large brass key in the door lock.

Alice-Miranda knocked on the door and then turned the tarnished brass handle. She wasn't sure what to expect but had in her mind something like the side sitting room at home, with its comfortable couches and television in the corner. This room, however, bore no resemblance to that one.

It was a large space with a threadbare maroon velvet chaise longue, just the right size for a child. There was also an impressive cedar bookcase which took up the entire length of the wall opposite the windows. A miniature pair of wingback chairs faced the garden, and in between them, on a low inlaid table, a tiny children's tea set in delicate blue-and-white china was laid out perfectly, as if guests were expected. Underneath one of the windows stood a huge Victorian doll's house and a white rocking horse. A wicker pram full of porcelain dolls completed the picture. Alice-Miranda noticed at once that, unlike the front hallway, there was not a speck of dust on the furniture, and she could see her reflection in the gleaming timber floor.

"I know someone's here. I'd really like to meet you," Alice-Miranda called as she walked around the room.

She reached into the pram and examined one of the china dolls. Its brilliant blue eyes opened and closed slowly when Alice-Miranda picked her up. "I need to talk to you. I'm lost and I have to find my way back to school!"

Alice-Miranda was sure she had seen with her own eyes the same figure dressed in black she'd spied earlier in the garden disappear into this room. Trouble was, there didn't seem to be any other doors, and there was certainly no one inside.

She checked behind the chairs and near the doll's house. The bookcase laden with hundreds of stories beckoned, and Alice-Miranda read the titles on the leather-bound spines. *Treasure Island* and *Alice in Wonderland* stood alongside *Moby-Dick* and *Great Expectations* and hundreds of other classics. Alice-Miranda walked along the length of glassed-in shelves before coming to an open section.

Reaching up to take a closer look, she put her hand on the slim volume of *Ali Baba and the Forty Thieves* and realized immediately that it wasn't a real book at all. It was made of wood, as was every other one beside it. Alice-Miranda knew that could mean only one thing.

She pushed and prodded every title along the line. It was only when she reached *Pride and Prejudice*, second from the last, that there was a loud click and the wall pivoted. It revealed a small windowless room containing a narrow single bed, a dressing table and a small sofa. A giant wardrobe stood against the far wall. Alice-Miranda could make out the sound of gentle weeping coming from inside.

"Please come out," Alice-Miranda soothed. "I really do need your help." She approached the wardrobe and turned the handle. As Alice-Miranda opened the door, there was a jagged scream and a tall figure within cowered, shielding its face.

"Please don't be afraid," Alice-Miranda begged.

She stepped back to allow whoever was inside the cupboard to come out. It was clearly an elderly woman, dressed in black from head to toe. Her blouse, long skirt, tights and shoes—all black—gave her the appearance of a bent stick of licorice. Atop her head was a black velvet bowler hat with a long black veil that reached down to her waist. The woman sniffed several times in quick sucession, then slowly stood up.

"Hello," Alice-Miranda said. "My name's Alice-Miranda Highton-Smith-Kennington-Jones and I'm very pleased to meet you, Miss . . ." Alice-Miranda extended her small hand.

The woman kept her head bowed and managed to

stumble from the cupboard, steadying herself on Alice-Miranda's outstretched arm.

"Do you have a name?" Alice-Miranda asked. "I'm so sorry if I startled you. I really just need some help. Why don't you come along with me and I'll make us both a nice cup of tea."

And with that, Alice-Miranda hurried away to the kitchen and busied herself finding the necessary ingredients to put the pot on. She was already pouring two cups of strong black tea when finally the woman appeared in the doorway.

"Oh, there you are." Alice-Miranda set the cups down at the kitchen table. "Please sit down. You still haven't told me your name though, miss, and I'd so like to know with whom I'm about to have tea."

The woman maneuvered her crooked frame into one of the antique timber chairs without a sound.

"I simply adore your house," Alice-Miranda continued. "It's terribly big and very beautiful, although I see perhaps you haven't had any help in the garden for a while. It's hard to keep such a huge place in check, isn't it? My mummy has an army of help and she still spends hours each week making sure things are just so. Do you live here on your own? Because that would be impossible . . . to keep on top of things, I mean. I'd so love to know your name."

Silence enveloped the house. Alice-Miranda grew aware of the ticking of a clock and glanced around the kitchen, searching for it.

"Aren't you afraid of me?" the woman asked quietly.

"Of course not." Alice-Miranda smiled. "Why would I be? In fact, I thought you seemed rather afraid of me—which is very silly indeed."

"Because . . ." The old woman faltered. "I'm the one . . . I'm the one they call the witch."

"Oh really? I had wondered about that. I met lots of cats on the way up here, and the girls at school told me a story a few nights ago about a witch in the woods with hundreds of cats, but I don't believe in witches. Everyone knows they're only in fairy stories—unless perhaps you really are a witch, in which case it's a pleasure to meet you, being the first real witch I've ever met." Alice-Miranda paused and sipped her tea. "Anyway, I really should tell you how I came to be here. You see, I was out riding with my best friend, Millie, and another friend Susannah and a new girl called Sloane and well, Sloane was riding Stumps and he's one of those ponies who you should never mention *home* to because, well, as soon as she did, he bolted and we all gave chase but my naughty little Bonaparte could smell your old vegetable patch and so they went one way and I went the other and that's how I ended up here at Caledonia Manor." Alice-Miranda finished her one-sided conversation and took another sip of tea.

"Oh," the woman said. There was a long pause. "My name's Hephzibah."

"What a delicious name." Alice-Miranda clapped her hands together. "I'm so glad we've met properly. Now we can truly be friends."

"Friends?" Hephzibah's voice quavered.

"Are you all right?" Alice-Miranda asked. "Why don't you take your hat off and then I can see you properly?"

"I can't," Hephzibah wheezed. "I can't."

"Of course you can," Alice-Miranda insisted. "I know it's important to wear sun protection outside, but we're inside, and I'd so love to see your face."

Hephzibah hesitated, fearing this would be a terrible mistake. But something about this child made her feel different. There was something comforting about her—something she hadn't felt since . . .

Hephzibah slowly lifted her veil before taking her hat off and placing it on the table beside her cup. She looked up at Alice-Miranda, her mouth drawn tightly into a thin line. With the fingers of her left hand, she gently traced the outline of her scarred face. A tear formed in her right eye and slid silently down her cheek, dropping onto her lap.

"Oh, you have such pretty eyes." Alice-Miranda smiled.

All at once, Hephzibah broke down into shuddering sobs. Alice-Miranda slipped from her seat, pulled the chair around beside her new friend, and immediately climbed up and placed her arm around the elderly woman's shoulder.

Chapter 17

Armed with a hand-drawn map tucked safely into her breast pocket, Alice-Miranda returned safely to school with Bonaparte that afternoon, to the great relief of all. Mr. Charles and Susannah had gone out in the Land Rover to look for her while Millie and Wally had taken the horses and retraced the girls' journey from Gertrude's Grove. Sloane said that there was no way she was going out looking for anyone—she had lines to learn (and a very sore bottom).

Alice-Miranda and Bony had met Millie and Wally at the fork in the road. She explained Bonaparte's willful behavior, saying that he had sniffed out an old vegetable patch and simply couldn't be held. Thankfully, she added, there weren't any cabbages, but she had pulled up a few woody carrots for Bony and then waited until he was in a better mood before heading for home. She didn't like telling untruths, but she had a feeling that the real story might cause undue concern.

Millie nodded after hearing her friend's tale. She well knew about Bonaparte's predilection for cabbages—and any other vegetable on offer.

Wally pointed toward the pathway where Bony and Alice-Miranda had come from. "You know, miss, the witch lives down there?"

"I'm sure there's no such thing, Wally," Alice-Miranda chided.

"It's true, you know. She's scary. I once went there with my mates—we was daring each other. It was just on dusk with the light fading fast and then we saw her—dressed from head to toe in black and this veil thing covering her ugly head. She screamed blue murder and set her feral cats on us. I ran so fast, I thought my heart was going to burst right out of my chest."

"Oh dear," Alice-Miranda whispered. "Poor Hephzibah."

"Anyway, looks like you survived, miss. Now, we'd

better get these ponies home. I'll call Charlie, and let him know you're safe and sound."

The group met at the stables. Alice-Miranda recounted the same story to Susannah and Charlie, who seemed satisfied with her explanation.

Millie, Alice-Miranda and Susannah walked back to the house.

"Well, you took your time getting back." Sloane glanced up at the girls from where she was lying on the couch in the sitting room, rehearsing her lines for the audition. "Did you have a fall?"

"Hello, Sloane," Alice-Miranda began. "I am sorry about the ride. I know I said that I wouldn't leave you at all, but my Bonaparte had other ideas, I'm afraid, and once he has a sniff of a vegetable patch, he's pretty much unstoppable."

"Well, now that I know how unreliable you are, I won't depend on you again." Sloane buried her head in the script.

Millie rolled her eyes. Susannah didn't say a word but headed straight to her room.

"Come on, Alice-Miranda," Millie said. "Let's go and get changed and then we can help each other learn our lines."

Sloane looked up and pouted. "I need someone to

practice with too. Jacinta's off doing stupid gymnastics training or something. Anyone would think she wants to go to the Olympics."

"She does," Millie replied.

"She does what?" asked Sloane, pulling a face.

"Want to go to the Olympics."

"She's incredible and I'm sure that she'll get there. She trains almost every day." Alice-Miranda smiled.

"Whatever." Sloane flicked her hand dismissively. "I need someone to rehearse with."

"We're busy," Millie informed Sloane as she grabbed her friend's hand and headed for their room.

"We could include Sloane, you know," Alice-Miranda said to Millie as they were getting changed.

"She's awful," Millie replied. "I thought Alethea was spoiled and horrible, but Sloane's just as foul."

"I'm sure she's just getting used to being at school, that's all," Alice-Miranda replied. "Don't you remember what it's like being the new girl?"

"Well, I hope I was never like her." Millie frowned.

Alice-Miranda and Millie spent the rest of the afternoon in all manner of poses and positions, learning their parts for the *Snow White and the Seven Dwarfs* auditions. Alice-Miranda decided she would try for the lead as well as some of the supporting roles, while Millie had her heart set on either Doc or the Magic Mirror.

Later that evening, Alice-Miranda skipped off to call her parents.

"Hello, Mummy, how are you?" she asked.

"I'm fine, darling—and how are you finding things back at school?" her mother fussed.

"Wonderful, Mummy—so please don't start crying. You know that I'm perfectly all right and if you cry, I won't call you anymore," Alice-Miranda scolded.

"Oh, don't be cross. Anyway, I have some marvelous news for you, sweetheart," her mother offered. "You know that Lawrence had made some inquiries about getting Lucas into Fayle? Well, first he was told that there were no spots at all and Lucas would have to go on the waiting list—which I think, between you and me, he didn't mind one bit. But Lawrence just called a little while ago and apparently there are twins leaving to do some traveling with their parents, so Lucas has a spot. He'll be starting next week. In fact, I think he might be there tomorrow afternoon."

"That's fantastic, Mummy. I can't wait to tell Jacinta. She'll be over the moon. Does that mean Aunt Charlotte and Lawrence will be bringing Lucas down? Will they have time to come and visit?" Alice-Miranda asked.

"Of course, darling. I'll phone Cha and let her know you're looking forward to seeing them."

Alice-Miranda wanted to tell her mother about Hephzibah, but something told her that now was not the right time. She knew that her parents would want to help, but she didn't know if Hephzibah was ready for the full force of the Highton-Smith-Kennington-Joneses just yet.

She had promised to visit Caledonia Manor again and knew that the only way she could go would be to take a friend with her, as students were not allowed to ride on their own. Of course she would take Millie, but she'd wait for just the right moment to tell her. Hephzibah hadn't asked to be kept a secret, but Alice-Miranda understood that there was something very special about her new friend—and just now, a strange feeling told her that their meeting would be best kept to herself.

Instead, she spent a few minutes telling her mother all about the excitement the play was causing. "I'd better go, Mummy. Millie and I are rehearsing for the auditions. I'd love to have a role—then I'll be able to see Lucas much more often."

"All right, darling. Love and hugs from Daddy and me, and Shilly just said to say hello and Dolly wants to know if you enjoyed the fudge."

Indeed, Alice-Miranda could hear Shilly and Mrs. Oliver calling out in the background.

"Tell Mrs. Oliver that her fudge was the best ever," Alice-Miranda replied. "Give everyone a big hug from me and I'll talk to you soon. Love you." She put the phone back into its cradle and ran off to find Jacinta and tell her the good news.

Chapter 18

In the late-afternoon sunshine, Smedley and September Sykes reclined on their brand-new lay-z lounges in their brand-new back garden, sipping brand-new champagne and indulging their fantasies about where they would take the children for vacation once Smedley's brand-new property developing business took off.

Although it wasn't the warmest of days, September was working on her tan, in a terrifyingly tiny leopard-print bikini. Smedley gazed admiringly at his wife, who he worried spent rather more time at the beauty salon than he could currently afford. Being a vacuum cleaner salesman, even on the home shopping channel, did not exactly bring in the big bucks. But Smedley believed with great certainty that their fortunes were about to change.

"Have you talked to the children today?" Smedley asked.

"Yes, Sloane called this morning. She's getting on soooo well with the other girls. I told her to make friends with that Highton-Smith-Kennington-Jones child. Imagine us being invited to their mansion for the weekend! They must be almost the richest people in the whole country," September babbled. "I haven't spoken to Sep, but I'm sure he's fine. I just hope he's making some friends—that boy needs to get his head out of those dull old science textbooks and start paying attention to the important things in life, like whose father owns that gorgeous sky-blue Rolls-Royce I saw turning out of the Fayle driveway when I was dropping Sloane at school the other day."

"Don't you worry about Septimus—he's just a bit shy, that's all. You keep working your magic, sweetheart, and I'm sure we'll be top of everyone's invitation list before long." Smedley grinned, revealing a dazzling white smile to match that of his wife's. A handsome man, Smedley had once harbored dreams of a career as a talk-show host. Unfortunately, things never quite happened the way he'd hoped and the closest he had come to being a TV star was plying his trade in vacuum cleaner technology on infomercials.

"You know, we'd be much farther up the social ladder if your father hadn't been such a dreadful cheapskate. The reading of his will was the most disappointing day of my life—fancy only leaving us his hideous old grocery shop and that poxy flat. I'd have thought a man of his supposed intelligence would have had some other investments," September moaned.

"Well, at least Stepmummy Henrietta's taken care of the school fees," Smedley said with a wink.

"Yes, I suppose so, but I wish that wretched nursing home would stop calling. You know I haven't got the time. I don't look like this"—September paused to bounce her curls—"by sitting on my rear end all day. There's the gym and the nail salon and the hairdresser and the beautician. And I think I should probably join the Village Women's Association too. I might be able to run some workshops for all the fashion victims around here." September rolled her huge blue eyes. "Golden Gates phoned four times yesterday. Apparently the daft old bat's been asking for some suitcase that was left in the shed at your father's place. I don't know where it is and I haven't got the time to go looking. I've no idea what happened to any of that rubbish. For all I know, it went to the dump."

Smedley sighed and stood up. As he stalked off toward the shed at the far end of the garden, his mobile phone rang. He disappeared into the shed and reemerged with a large blue suitcase in his left hand, all the while continuing his conversation.

September could only hear snatches of the exchange.

"Yes, yes, that's great. How much? Fantastic, I'll put the money in the account tomorrow." Her husband gave her the thumbs-up, then strode back toward the terrace, where she was sitting.

September sat up. "What was all that, then?"

"Everything's a go for the offshore property deal." Smedley put the suitcase down by the back door before picking up the champagne bottle and topping up both their glasses. "Won't be long now until we're living life in the fast lane." He raised his glass and tried to chink it against September's, except that it thudded instead, being made of plastic. "And I think that's Stepmummy Henrietta's suitcase." He pointed at the battered leather bag.

"Well, I haven't got time to deliver it. You'll have to take it. And you'd better be right about this deal, because I have just bought two pairs of designer jeans and a gorgeous leather jacket—and someone has to pay for them. I've got my eye on a new fridge with a built-in ice-maker, and you know we *have* to buy a fountain for the garden. I can't possibly work anymore, what with the children and their hectic schedules," September griped.

Smedley had rather hoped that now that Septimus and Sloane were busy at boarding school, September might get a few odd modeling jobs here and there—but after what had happened earlier in the year, he was reluctant to bring up the subject again.

A few months ago Smedley had heard about a new agency that was recruiting and had been stupid enough to read the ad aloud to her. "Models required! All ages, sizes, shapes and talents welcome."

September had gone very white for a moment and then flown into a blistering red rage. "You might as well say I'm a fat old cow with a head like a buzzard! Is that what you mean, Smedley?" she had screamed.

"No, darling, of course not. It's just that, well, you're not quite the little thing you were before the children, now, are you? And I hear there's very good money in catalog work for the more mature lady."

Smedley had dug himself a hole that took two whole months to get out of. No end of flowers and shoes, and shoes and handbags, and handbags and flowers had been able to thaw September's icy mood until one day he walked into the kitchen and threw a set of car keys on the counter.

"For you, darling." He looked at the keys and glanced up at his wife.

"If you think getting my car washed is going to see you back in the good books, Smedley Sykes, then you're even thicker than I thought."

"Have a look at the keys, my lovely," Smedley cooed. "I think you might find that the 'car wash' had rather a transforming effect."

September picked up the keys. She examined them carefully and realized that the key ring certainly wasn't that of her old sedan.

"Oh my gosh, Smedley, what have you done?" September squealed. "Is it new?"

"Of course, darling. Nothing less would do for you, my sweetheart." Smedley laid on the charm so thick you could have eaten it on toast for breakfast. He held out his arms, waiting for September to rush into his embrace. His wife, however, had other priorities, and ran straight past her husband to the garage to hug her new baby sports car.

Smedley had hoped that would do the trick and might even encourage September to give the modeling another thought. Goodness knows, the jobs were hardly taxing and usually paid more money than he saw in a month. But she would have none of it, and he hadn't been brave enough to mention it again, although he was thinking about it—a lot.

Smedley sat back down beside his wife and pushed his sunglasses onto the top of his head.

"Smedley, is this deal really going to come off?" September glared. "I'm so sick of being poor. I just don't deserve this life," she wailed.

"Don't you worry your pretty head, my lovely. Soon enough the Sykeses will have more money than God."

September smiled broadly. "But how do you know how much money God has?" she asked, tilting her head and looking thoughtful.

"Oh, trust me, darling—I'm sure he has loads," said Smedley.

Chapter 19

The Fayle school campus spread out over a thousand glistening acres, with magnificent Victorian buildings surrounded by sports fields, a swimming pool, a sailing lake and stables. From the road it was almost completely hidden from view, no doubt the result of clever planning by generations of gardeners. McGlintock Manor, named after its founder's beloved wife, Helena Louise McGlintock, was renowned as the most beautiful of any school building in the country and had been extended over the years to house most of the classrooms and administration areas and the headmaster's residence.

Septimus could hardly believe his luck when he

heard that his stepgrandmother Henrietta had arranged for him and his sister Sloane to go to boarding school. It had been his dream—and one that he'd shared with his beloved grandfather Percy on the rare occasions that he'd been allowed to visit and the even rarer ones he'd been able to stay the night. Three years ago, Septimus had pinned a list of schools he would have liked to attend to his bedroom wall, with Fayle being his first preference. He'd heard that it was an outstanding institution, where being smart was revered rather than reviled. And if there was one thing Septimus most certainly was, it was smart.

In his family, Sep had always felt like the odd one out. The only person who truly understood him was Grandpa Percy, and now that he was gone, life seemed like a lonely place. Septimus adored reading—about science and history and politics. His mother, on the other hand, only ever flicked through the pages of *Women's Daily* and *Gloss and Goss,* his father pored over the racing pages at the back of the newspaper, and his sister thought reading was something you only ever did if the television was on the blink. He loved his mother and father, but quite simply, he thought they could have been from another planet.

{119}

So when Septimus arrived at Fayle, he found that it was even better than he had dreamt of. Although just twelve years of age, Sep had learned early the difference between what you hoped for and what you expected. While he hoped the students would be kind, the teachers brilliant and the school perfect, what he expected was very different.

At his last school, on the very first day the kids had branded him Septic Sykes, and it had stuck. He expected the teachers at his new school to be strict in the extreme, perhaps even carrying canes or some other medieval devices of punishment. But so far, Fayle was different. No one said anything about his name. When he told the boys that everyone called him Sep, they believed him without question and Sep it was. And the teachers, while perhaps a little on the vague side, were incredibly knowledgeable and kind, with no sign of any instruments of torture. He couldn't believe that there was absolutely nothing to be disappointed about—and that made him happier than he had been in his entire life.

Now that he was a full-fledged member of Fayle, Septimus vowed to make the most of every minute. Within the first few days, he'd signed up for the school newspaper, the science club, the athletics squad and swimming training. At assembly, Professor Winterbottom announced that, for the first time in over ten years, Fayle would be teaming up with the girls from Winchesterfield-Downsfordvale to put on a play. Drama wasn't something he had any experience with, but he was willing to give it a go all the same.

On Saturday afternoon, Sep was on his way to the running track when the headmaster called out to him from across the quadrangle.

"I'd like a word, young man." The professor walked toward him, peering over the top of his spectacles.

Professor Wallace Winterbottom had been the headmaster at Fayle for a very long time. The school was his life and, although his long-suffering wife, Deidre, often hinted that she thought it might be time they took off and saw the world, Wallace was deaf to her suggestions. Deidre enjoyed school life too, but carried a long-held desire to visit the pyramids and Greece. In fact, she had an extensive list of places she wanted to see, which curiously enough she carried with her everywhere, in her right shoe.

The three loves of Wallace's life were Fayle, of course, his beloved West Highland Terrier named Parsley, and his wife, Deidre, possibly even in that order. He had started his teaching career at Fayle as a young English master and gained the role of head

{121}

very early on. So, in all, he'd been at the school for more than forty years—almost a record, but not quite. Hedges, the gardener, beat him by a long shot, having started at age fourteen; he was now seventy-four and showing no signs at all of slowing down.

"Yes, sir," Septimus replied as he reached the old man.

"We've got a new boy starting tomorrow and I was thinking he might go in with you," Professor Winterbottom began. "Name's Lucas Nixon. He's had a rough trot lately, so I need someone who'll look after the lad. Can I rely on you?"

Sep nodded. "Of course, sir. I'd be pleased to have a roommate. It's been a bit quiet."

"Very good. That will be all." The professor came as close to a smile as anyone might ever have seen.

Septimus was looking forward to the arrival of a roommate. He'd already made friends with several of the boys, and although he enjoyed his own company, it would be good to have someone to talk to after lights-out.

Chapter 20

"Guess who starts at Fayle tomorrow?" It was now Saturday evening and Alice-Miranda and Millie had just joined Jacinta in the dining room dinner line.

"Lucas?" Jacinta asked, wide-eyed.

The other girls nodded.

Jacinta gasped. "That's fantastic. I can't wait to see him."

Millie rolled her eyes. "Three weeks ago, you couldn't stand him. Now I think you've got a serious crush."

"No, I don't," Jacinta protested. "We just under-stand each other, that's all."

"Well, I don't think we'll get to see Lucas tomorrow." Alice-Miranda shuffled along, edging closer to where Mrs. Smith was pushing out plates of steaming hot roast beef, crispy potatoes, beans and cauliflower cheese covered with lashings of thick gravy. "But Mummy said that she would see if Aunt Charlotte and Lawrence can pop in and say hello once they've got Lucas settled."

"Ohhhh," Jacinta sighed. "Imagine, Lawrence Ridley—here—at Winchesterfield-Downsfordvale. Best keep that between us or the poor man will be mobbed. He's sooo dreamy."

Millie and Alice-Miranda giggled.

"I'm sure you'll look after him, Jacinta." Millie grinned.

"Yes, of course I will. He's a national treasure and in my favorite ever movie."

The girls hadn't noticed Sloane, who had slipped into the line behind Millie and was eavesdropping on their conversation.

"Did you say Lawrence Ridley?" Sloane asked. "As in Lawrence Ridley, the movie star?"

"Oh, hello there, Sloane." Alice-Miranda leaned around Jacinta and Millie so that she could see her. "Yes, that's right. Jacinta did say Lawrence Ridley."

"How do you know him?" Sloane demanded. "If you actually do, that is."

"Oh yes, I really do. We all do. Lawrence is my aunt Charlotte's fiancé and his son Lucas is starting at Fayle tomorrow. Do you remember I told you about them when we were out riding this morning?" Alice-Miranda smiled.

"No, you didn't. You didn't say anything about Lawrence Ridley. I'd have remembered that," Sloane replied.

"Well, I thought I did, but perhaps I didn't. Anyway, he's the loveliest fellow and terribly handsome too."

"Will I get to meet him?" Sloane demanded.

"Quite possibly, if he and Aunt Charlotte come over tomorrow once they've dropped Lucas off." Alice-Miranda picked up her knife and fork as the group moved down the counter.

"You have to introduce me," Sloane insisted. "Meeting Lawrence Ridley is definitely on my to-do list."

"You're well organized, having a to-do list. Oh, hello, Mrs. Smith." Alice-Miranda reached the front of the line. "It looks like you've outdone yourself tonight. Dinner smells delicious." She picked up her plate and held it under her nose. "And thank you for the picnic today—it was scrumptious. That chocolate cake was one of the best ever."

"My pleasure. Dolly gave me a few pointers with my cauliflower cheese, so I'm hoping that it's up to scratch. I know there's no one makes it like she does, but I am trying." Mrs. Smith pushed forward another plate, which Millie scooped up.

Alice-Miranda nodded. "I think it looks perfect."

Mrs. Smith smiled. It seemed to be her automatic response whenever Alice-Miranda appeared.

The girls moved off to find a table. Sloane followed rather more closely than Jacinta was comfortable with.

"Are you going to sit with us, Sloane?" Alice-Miranda turned and asked her. "You're most welcome."

Millie and Jacinta exchanged frowns.

Sloane gave a halfhearted nod. Although she would have preferred to be with some of the older girls, she wanted to find out more about Lawrence Ridley. It really didn't seem fair at all that the painful little brat would end up with a movie star for an uncle.

The dining room hummed as girls swapped stories of their day. Alice-Miranda was so pleased to see Miss Grimm and Mr. Grump sitting with Mr. Plumpton and Miss Reedy, chatting and smiling. Mr.

Plumpton's red nose glowed like a beacon as he roared laughing at something Mr. Grump had just shared with the group. This was exactly what school should be like, she thought. But there was something worrying her too, and it was all to do with her new friend Hephzibah.

Sloane interrupted her thoughts. "So what's he really like?"

"Who?" Alice-Miranda looked up from where she had just pushed her knife through a plump potato.

"Lawrence Ridley, of course." Sloane rolled her eyes. "Don't you ever listen?"

"Oh, he's a darling," Alice-Miranda replied.

"But what else?" Sloane quizzed.

"What do you mean, what else?" Alice-Miranda asked.

"Well, he's a movie star. He must have loads of girlfriends and go to parties all the time and get himself into lots of trouble," Sloane purred.

"No, I don't think so. He's really just an ordinary person," said Alice-Miranda. "More handsome than the average fellow, but perfectly normal, as far as I can tell."

Sloane sneered. She was clearly disappointed by Alice-Miranda's response. "Well, he doesn't sound like any of the movie stars I know," she huffed.

{127}

"And who do you know?" Millie queried.

Sloane glared at Millie. "Loads of people."

"Really? Such as?" Millie invited.

"You wouldn't know them." Sloane picked up her plate and stalked off to sit at another table.

"You know she's lying." Millie shook her head. "I'm sure she doesn't know anyone."

"Give her a chance, Millie," Alice-Miranda replied. "She's just trying to fit in."

Toward the end of the meal, Miss Reedy stood up from her seat and moved to the podium.

"Ahem." She cleared her throat. "Girls, I just wanted to remind you all that auditions will commence tomorrow afternoon at two p.m. in the Great Hall. The schedule has been posted on the notice-board. Please take note of the time you have been allocated and don't be late, as we have a lot to get through."

"That's so exciting!" Alice-Miranda gasped when Miss Reedy finished her speech.

"Yes, let's just hope that you-know-who doesn't get the main role." Jacinta nodded toward Sloane, who had taken her dessert off to yet another table. "Her head's big enough already."

Alice-Miranda came to Sloane's defense. "If she

does, she'll have earned it. You know Miss Reedy doesn't play favorites."

The girls finished their butterscotch pudding and raced off to check the time of their auditions. Millie ran her finger down the list, finding Alice-Miranda at 2:30 p.m., Jacinta at 2:45 p.m. and her own name at 3:00 p.m.

"I'd better let Mummy know to tell Aunt Charlotte not to come until afternoon tea time so we can all be finished," Alice-Miranda said as the three girls skipped back to Grimthorpe House and an early night.

Chapter 21

An hour after lights out, Alice-Miranda lay awake in bed, her mind a whirl. She was excited about the auditions tomorrow, but there was something else. She couldn't stop thinking about Hephzibah. She knew her friend wasn't ready for one of her parents' rescue missions—not just yet. Alice-Miranda wanted to visit again in the morning, but she couldn't go riding on her own. It wasn't allowed, and for good reason too. There was only one thing for it. She had to tell Millie.

"Millie," she whispered. "Are you awake?"

Millie rolled over and faced her friend. "Yes, I thought *you* were asleep. I've been trying to remember my lines and now I can't stop thinking about them."

"I can't sleep either—but it's not because of the auditions. I have to tell you something, but you must promise not to tell anyone else. It's terribly important."

"Of course," Millie replied as she wriggled out from under the covers and propped herself against her pillow.

Alice-Miranda sat up and hugged her knees under her chin. A shard of moonlight fell through the window, creating a soft half-light.

"What is it?" Millie looked at her friend. She couldn't remember Alice-Miranda ever looking so serious.

"Well, you know this afternoon when Bonaparte bolted?" Alice-Miranda began.

"Yes, the little monster. I think that pony of yours has bionic smell power." Millie giggled at her own joke.

"That's for sure. But it's just that I didn't tell you the whole story," Alice-Miranda continued.

Millie raised her eyebrows. "The whole story?"

"I met someone, and they helped me find my way back to the fork in the path."

"Who was it?" Millie asked. "Was it a gypsy or a tramp or someone?"

{131}

"No, of course not." Alice-Miranda shook her head.

"Well, why are you being so secretive about it?" Millie frowned. "Did they hurt you?"

"Goodness, no!" Alice-Miranda gasped. "We're friends. I want to go and visit her again tomorrow, and I'd like you to come with me."

"Of course I will," Millie replied. "We'll go early, just after breakfast.

"You must promise that you won't be scared," Alice-Miranda added.

"Why would I be scared if she's your friend?"

"Well, it's just that there are stories. You see, she has a rather large number of cats."

Millie's eyes widened. "No!" she gasped. "You didn't. . . ."

Chapter 22

"Are you going riding *again?*" Jacinta moaned as Alice-Miranda and Millie arrived at the breakfast table dressed in their jodhpurs, shirts and boots. Millie placed her plate down opposite Jacinta while Alice-Miranda slid in next to her.

Ignoring the question, Millie looked up and asked Jacinta if she was training that morning.

"Of course," she replied.

"Then why are you whining about us going riding?" Millie frowned. "You don't have time to play anyway."

"Oh, good point." Jacinta took a mouthful of cereal.

"Hello, Sloane." Alice-Miranda smiled as the school's newest student set her plate down at the end of their table.

"Don't expect me to come riding with you two again," Sloane grouched when she noticed the way Alice-Miranda and Millie were dressed. "After what you did yesterday, I'll wait until Hugo arrives, thank you very much."

"Well, for your information, we weren't going to ask you anyway," Millie replied. "And I thought you said that your horse was called Harry?"

"No, I didn't." Sloane narrowed her eyes. "You just don't listen." She stuck her nose in the air, picked up her plate and headed off to sit with Ivory and Ashima, who didn't exactly look pleased to see her.

The girls tucked into their breakfast.

"Yum, that was delicious." Alice-Miranda licked her lips. "I love Sundays—Mrs. Smith always does something extra yummy."

Millie stabbed at the last piece of pancake on her plate and popped it into her mouth.

"We should get going," Alice-Miranda suggested. "We don't want to be late getting back."

"If we come back." Millie raised her eyebrows meaningfully.

"What's that supposed to mean?" Jacinta quizzed.

"Nothing." Alice-Miranda smiled. "Millie's just being dramatic. Isn't that one of the lines in your audition piece?"

"Ha ha!" Millie replied, her face deadly serious.

"I'll see you both later, then." Jacinta scraped the last of her cornflakes from the bowl before starting on her pancakes.

"Bye," Millie gulped.

"See you soon, Jacinta," Alice-Miranda called.

The two girls headed for the stables, where they promptly set about saddling Bony and Chops. It was Wally's day off so, in accordance with school rules, Alice-Miranda scratched a note on the old chalkboard which hung at the building's entrance, saying what time they were heading out and when they thought they'd be back. It was also one of the rules to say where they were going. Without wanting to lie, Alice-Miranda jotted down—*Millie and Alice-Miranda, same as yesterday.*

The girls mounted their ponies and walked lazily out of the stable block and into the warm morning sunshine.

"You must have had a good sleep, Bonaparte—you do seem to be in a better mood today." Alice-Miranda squeezed her legs and the pony sprang to life, jogging down the path toward the gate which led to the forest beyond the school's boundaries. Millie was unusually quiet as she trotted alongside her friend.

Finally, she spoke. "Are you sure she's not . . . you know?" Millie asked for at least the tenth time since Alice-Miranda had shared her secret the night before.

"Millie, I promise, she's not. But if you don't want to come in, you don't have to," Alice-Miranda reassured her.

Millie wanted to believe her tiny friend. But she'd heard the story about the witch a few times since she started at the school. It was hard to believe that it wasn't true. Deep down, she wasn't sure if she actually believed in witches at all, but the witch in the woods had been folklore at Winchesterfield-Downsfordvale for generations.

The girls continued through the woods, following the map Hephzibah had drawn for Alice-Miranda the day before.

As they approached the estate, Bony thrust his nose in the air and whinnied. Alice-Miranda held the reins as tightly as she could. "I don't think so, mister—you're not running off today. There are no vegetables in that old patch anyway." Alice-Miranda guided Millie toward the first set of gates, which yesterday had been a passing blur. Two limestone pillars, an indication of the grandeur of the estate contained within, towered next to an unwieldy yew hedge. The rusted gates, held hostage by years of untended foliage, bore an intricate pattern.

"Look at that." Alice-Miranda pulled on the reins and Bonaparte stopped in the middle of the entrance. "Can you see that, Millie?" She pointed at the gate on the left-hand side. "It looks like a giant *C* wrapped into the iron."

Millie nodded, too in awe to speak.

"Oh, and look there, on the other gate—there's an *M* . . . *CM*—of course, Caledonia Manor! Gosh, someone went to a lot of trouble with this place," Alice-Miranda prattled.

"And look at that." Millie's voice trembled. There was a weathered sign covered with vines poking out of the bushes. It read, KEEP OUT! TRESPASSERS WILL BE PROSECUTED.

"Are you sure we should go in?"

"Of course," Alice-Miranda replied. "Don't pay any attention to that silly old thing."

The girls continued on their journey up the overgrown drive, past the ancient vegetable patch with its weedy scarecrows. The ponies clip-clopped toward the dilapidated stable block with its missing slates and grimy walls. A black cat with huge green eyes appeared on the top of the outer wall and was immediately joined by three of his friends—a ginger, a tabby and a gray.

"Good morning, pussycats," Alice-Miranda addressed the row of felines. They responded with a cacophony of meows. "How sweet—a welcome song from the Kitty Chorus," Alice-Miranda giggled.

It didn't even raise a grin from Millie. Her mouth seemed plastered shut as she took in their surroundings.

"We'll leave the ponies here." Alice-Miranda slid down off Bonaparte and took the reins forward over his head. She scrounged around in her pocket for a sugar cube, which Bony nibbled from her outstretched hand.

Millie found her voice. "Why can't we ride the whole way?"

"I think it's safer to tie them up here than somewhere near the house. This is where I left Bony yesterday," Alice-Miranda replied. "I don't want him getting any more ideas about that vegetable patch. It's perfectly safe."

Millie hopped down from the saddle and followed Alice-Miranda into the outside stall. Both girls looped their reins through the bridles so the ponies could move freely around the yard. A heavy overnight downpour had half-filled a smooth stone water trough in the corner that Bonaparte rushed straight for.

"Are you sure they'll be all right?" Millie followed Alice-Miranda out of the enclosure.

"Positive." Her friend nodded, checking the latch. "It's not too far to the main house. Just wait until you see it, Millie—it's amazing."

Millie was not convinced. So far, the stables and the gardens looked like a picture from one of her old Grimm's fairy tale books. She seemed to recall that the owner of *that* house had some rather nasty magical powers.

Alice-Miranda took off up the drive with Millie in tow. This time, the cats from the stables seemed happy to stay where they were, lolling about in the sunshine, keeping one eye on their equine friends.

As the girls reached the second set of gates, Alice-Miranda noticed that the ivy she'd pulled from the gatepost only the day before had already begun to reattach itself to the brass nameplate.

"Caledonia Manor? More like Creepy Manor if you ask me," Millie muttered under her breath as she looked around at the fossilized garden urns and enormous derelict fountain overgrown with weeds. She half expected a giant or troll or some other fairy-tale creature to emerge from the thicket beside them at any moment.

The girls rounded the final bend and there in all its tumbledown splendor was Caledonia Manor. Millie gasped as Alice-Miranda had done the day before. "It's huge," she breathed.

"Yes, it's amazing, isn't it?" Alice-Miranda replied. "Such a lovely house."

"Lovely?" Millie questioned. "I can think of some other words that would better describe this place."

"Oh, I know it's far from perfect," Alice-Miranda began, "but if you look past the flaky paint and the grubby windowpanes, there's a real beauty underneath."

Millie was not so sure. The house was enormous, that was true. But as for beautiful, she was not at all convinced.

"Come on," Alice-Miranda called as she ran toward one side of the building.

Millie gasped again when the girls emerged from the tangled undergrowth and onto the open lawn at the rear of the house.

Alice-Miranda continued on her way, jogging up the stone steps with their zigzag balustrade. "Hurry up," she called. Millie's heart hammered in her chest.

Her mouth was dry, as if she'd eaten a bucket of rocks.

Alice-Miranda reached the back porch and waited for Millie to catch up.

Five black cats lazed in various positions along the terrace. Millie hesitated when she saw them. She was quite convinced their eyes were following her every move.

"I might wait here," Millie gulped.

"Oh, all right, if you're sure." Alice-Miranda tapped on the glass panel of the kitchen door. There was no answer. "But I might be a little while."

"Wait, I'll come." Millie ran to stand beside her friend.

Alice-Miranda knocked again, then turned the handle and walked into the kitchen.

"Helloooo?" she called. "Are you here, Miss Hephzibah? It's me, Alice-Miranda. I've come to visit and I've brought a friend."

The door to the room off the kitchen, which Alice-Miranda thought of as the playroom, was closed. There was a rustling sound coming from within. The tiny child knocked gently and called again. Then she opened the door and poked her head inside.

Millie stood on the other side of the kitchen. In

spite of the warmth of the day, she shivered beside the lit stove.

"Hello, Miss Hephzibah," Alice-Miranda called. "I'm going to put the pot on, and I've brought some lovely cake for your morning tea."

Millie tried to see inside the room but her feet seemed set in concrete.

"If you'd rather take your tea in here," Alice-Miranda continued, "I can bring it in for you in a minute."

From where she stood, Millie heard no reply. Alice-Miranda closed the door and walked back across the kitchen, where she busied herself filling a battered copper kettle, which she placed on the stove top.

Millie hadn't moved an inch. "Is she . . . is she in there?" Millie whispered.

"Oh yes. I think she's feeling a little tired, so I said that I would take the tea in for her." Alice-Miranda smiled. "Are you all right? You look a bit pale."

Millie's freckly face had drained of color. Her red hair looked like firelight against her porcelain skin.

"Are you really going in there?" Millie pointed at the closed door.

"Of course. Will you come with me?" Alice-Miranda asked as she removed three china cups and saucers from the pine sideboard.

Millie shook her head.

"That's all right. You can stay here if you'd prefer."

Millie's eyes darted all over the place as she took in the kitchen and its ancient contents. There was another doorway to her left and a further entranceway at the opposite end of the room.

"There's a back staircase just through that door beside you." Alice-Miranda filled the teapot with boiling water. "I went upstairs yesterday, but I haven't had a proper look around because I heard a clatter down here, and that's when I found Miss Hephzibah. I was rather hoping we might be able to explore properly sometime."

Millie peered at the doorway. Her mind raced. Perhaps it was safer to join Alice-Miranda in the other room. She didn't fancy being alone in the cavernous kitchen with its creaks and groans and doors to who-knows-where.

"I'll come," Millie blurted.

"That's lovely. But you mustn't be frightened. Other than me yesterday, I don't think Miss Hephzibah has seen anyone for a long time, and she's very shy." Alice-Miranda poured three cups of black tea. From her backpack she produced a container of milk and three large slices of butter cake. When she'd asked Mrs. Smith for three pieces this morning, the cook had automatically assumed that Millie and Alice-Miranda were taking one of the other girls with them on their ride. Alice-Miranda hadn't corrected her.

"Is that a tray over there?" Alice-Miranda pointed at a cabinet next to where Millie was still rooted to the spot.

Millie spun around, moving for the first time since the girls had entered the kitchen. She bent down and retrieved an ornate timber tray, its faded decoration hinting at the once grand house's glory days. She handed it to Alice-Miranda, who loaded it up with the three cups and plates.

"Can you open the door for me, please?" Alice-Miranda picked up the tray and walked toward the playroom door.

"Oh." Millie swallowed hard. "Okay." She walked forward slowly as if at any moment she might turn and flee.

"It's all right, really it is," Alice-Miranda reassured Millie as she reached up and turned the handle.

Chapter 23

That afternoon, Millie, Jacinta and Alice-Miranda milled about outside the assembly hall, waiting for their turn to audition. Millie and Alice-Miranda couldn't help exchange knowing glances as they recalled their morning's adventure. Fortunately, Jacinta was far too engrossed in reading over her lines to notice their strange looks. Ashima emerged from the building.

"How did you do?" Alice-Miranda asked.

"Okay, I think. You can go in now, Alice-Miranda. Miss Reedy asked for you. Good luck."

"Thanks!" Alice-Miranda bounced into the hall.

"Hello there, young lady." Miss Reedy smiled. "I

see you're auditioning for two parts this afternoon. May I introduce Mr. Lipp?" Miss Reedy nodded at the gentleman sitting beside her. They each had a pile of papers in front of them. Mr. Lipp was dressed in a very dapper mustard-colored suit with a multicolored tie. His handlebar mustache was neatly groomed; however, his eyebrows resembled two hairy caterpillars crawling across his brow.

"Hello, Mr. Lipp." Alice-Miranda walked toward him and held out her hand across the table. "My name is Alice-Miranda Highton-Smith-Kennington-Jones and I'm very pleased to meet you, sir."

Mr. Lipp peered over the top of his spectacles and gently shook Alice-Miranda's tiny hand. "Pleased to meet you too, young lady."

"Now, where shall we start?" Miss Reedy glanced at the list in front of her.

"If I may, Miss Reedy, I'd like to read for Snow White first." Alice-Miranda walked up the side steps and onto the stage.

"Very well," Miss Reedy agreed. "Why don't you commence from the part where the huntsman is taking Snow White into the forest with the intention of killing her. That should give you a bit of dramatic scope."

Alice-Miranda stood in the middle of the stage and

gathered her thoughts. She imagined that the assembly hall was now a dark forest and that the hunter was standing right in front of her.

"Please, sir, don't kill me. If you let me go, I promise I'll tell no one. I will find somewhere to live and I won't ever return to the palace," Alice-Miranda pleaded with her imaginary foe.

Miss Reedy read the part of the huntsman. "But I . . . I have a job to do. The Queen will—"

"Sir!" Alice-Miranda interrupted before letting out a heart-wrenching sob. "I beg you." The tiny child fell to her knees.

"Then go. Go far away and never return. I will take the Queen the heart of a boar and make her believe that it was yours," Miss Reedy read passionately.

Alice-Miranda looked up slowly. "Thank you, kind sir. Thank you with all my heart. Your generosity will never be forgotten." And with that, Alice-Miranda fled into the wings.

Mr. Lipp brushed his eye and sniffed. Miss Reedy threw him a curious glance and he at once protested, "Dust, I think. Yes, very dusty in here." He stuck his finger in his eye as if to remove the offending object.

Alice-Miranda returned to the stage, and both Mr. Lipp and Miss Reedy clapped vigorously.

"Well done, my dear, that was wonderful," Miss Reedy enthused.

"Thank you." Alice-Miranda smiled and gave a little bow. "May I read for the part of the narrator now?" she asked.

Mr. Lipp and Miss Reedy lowered their voices.

"No, I don't think so," said Mr. Lipp finally.

"But, Mr. Lipp, I'd like to give myself a chance as the narrator."

"Alice-Miranda, there's no need. You're the final girl auditioning for the part of Snow White and we've decided that the role shall be yours," Miss Reedy announced. "But if you would please keep that to yourself until the cast is announced on Wednesday, we'd greatly appreciate it." She raised her eyebrows and then paused, thinking. "Unless, of course, Mr. Lipp, you have any boys who have put their names down for that role? I'd almost forgotten. We still have to see the Fayle boys tomorrow afternoon."

"Ahem." Mr. Lipp cleared his throat. "No, I don't know of any boys who have expressed a desire to play the role of Snow White." He grinned. "Although, last year when we were flying solo on the school play, one of the lads did a very good job of Maid Marian in Robin Hood."

Alice-Miranda giggled. Miss Reedy did too.

"It looks like the part's yours, young lady." Miss Reedy nodded. "But"—the teacher raised her forefinger to her lip—"until Wednesday."

"Of course, Miss Reedy. Thank you so much. I promise I won't let you down." Alice-Miranda skipped out of the hall and raced off to meet Millie and Jacinta, who were waiting outside.

Chapter 24

"I am a complete failure," Jacinta wailed. "Mr. Lipp didn't appreciate my improvisations of Happy turning cartwheels at all. He said that, as far as he knew, dwarfs weren't renowned for their gymnastic abilities."

"Don't worry, Jacinta. I'm sure you did just fine," Alice-Miranda comforted her friend. "And you auditioned for the role of the narrator as well, didn't you?"

"Yes." Jacinta pouted. "I couldn't even tell what Miss Reedy and Mr. Lipp thought about *that*."

"There's always stage crew," Millie added.

"Stage crew—for losers who couldn't get a proper part in the play," Jacinta moaned.

"No, that's not true, Jacinta. The stage crew is very important. If there weren't a stage crew, then the actors would have to slip in and out of character as they carried trees and buildings and magic mirrors and things on and off the stage. Just imagine—the Evil Queen finishes her lines and then has to pick up the mirror and struggle off with it—that would be terribly silly." Alice-Miranda grinned.

"I suppose you're right." Jacinta managed a half-smile. "Hopefully I'll get a part, but if I don't, stage crew will have to do."

"What about you, Millie, did your audition go well?" Alice-Miranda asked.

"I think so. I'm not sure which part I'd prefer, though. Doc's pretty funny, but I love that the Magic Mirror gets to give it to the Queen," Millie replied. "How do you think you did, Alice-Miranda?"

"Okay, I think," she replied.

The girls were on their way to the front of the school to meet Charlotte and Lawrence, who had phoned to say they would be at Winchesterfield-Downsfordvale in time for afternoon tea. Sloane was stalking about in the garden.

"Oh, hello, Sloane," Alice-Miranda called when she spotted her lurking behind the rosebushes. "What are you doing over there?"

Sloane looked up. "I was just, um, waiting for my mother," she replied. "She's coming to visit."

"That's convenient," Millie whispered to Jacinta. "More likely she told her that Lawrence was stopping by. She'd better not cause a scene."

"Why don't you come over here and wait with us?" Alice-Miranda asked.

Millie and Jacinta huffed.

Sloane walked over to the group.

"Did you enjoy your audition?" Alice-Miranda asked.

"I suppose so," Sloane replied.

"What did you try out for?" Jacinta asked.

"The only role worth having, of course," she scoffed.

Alice-Miranda felt a flurry of butterflies in her tummy. Sloane would be very disappointed when she missed out on the part of Snow White.

"So you tried out for Snow White, then?" Millie pressed.

"Good grief, no," Sloane replied. "Who'd want to be that sappy little do-gooder? I'm going to be the Evil Queen. That's the only part that's any good in this pathetic little fairy tale."

Alice-Miranda exhaled softly. Her butterflies flapped their wings and flew right away.

In the distance, the girls could hear the low rumble of a sports car engine. A shiny silver vehicle entered the driveway.

"They're here!" Alice-Miranda ran down the steps of Winchesterfield Manor to greet her beloved aunt and soon-to-be uncle.

"Oh my gosh, it's really him!" Sloane gasped.

"Of course it is," Jacinta replied. "Did you think Alice-Miranda was making it up?"

"No," Sloane spat. "I believed her."

The car grumbled to a halt in one of the recently added visitor parking spaces. Only a matter of months ago, parents and other family members were strictly forbidden from visiting the school at any time other than to drop off and pick up their daughters at the beginning and end of term. But of course, that had all changed now, and Miss Grimm had come to see the importance of family dropping in whenever possible.

"Hello!" Alice-Miranda launched herself at her aunt Charlotte as soon as she was out of the car.

Charlotte scooped the little child into her arms and peppered her face with kisses—cheeks, forehead and, lastly, the tip of Alice-Miranda's nose. It had been done that way for as long as either of them could remember. Alice-Miranda hugged her tightly.

"And how is my favorite niece?" Charlotte set the child down. Lawrence emerged from the rear of the car and snuck up behind Alice-Miranda, tickling her wildly before twirling her over his shoulder and depositing her back on the ground.

She squealed with delight. "I'm . . . very . . . well . . . thank . . . you," Alice-Miranda gasped between giggles.

Millie chuckled and Jacinta almost fainted.

"Hello, Millie and Jacinta." Charlotte ran up the steps and kissed both girls on the cheek. Lawrence followed, with Alice-Miranda holding tight to his left hand.

"And how are my favorite adopted nieces?" He leaned down and hugged Millie, then Jacinta. Jacinta's legs turned to jelly.

"Great, thanks, Mr. Ridley," Millie replied. Jacinta said nothing but stood looking rather goggle-eyed. A quick jab to the ribs from Millie seemed to bring her back around.

"Well, very, thank you." Jacinta shook her head. "I mean, very well, thank you."

Sloane had remained a few steps away from the group, taking it all in. She wished she really had phoned her mother to come and see this. In fact, she knew she'd be in huge trouble for not telling her. It was just that her mother had a way of making it all about her, and this was Sloane's opportunity to meet a real live movie star without her mother being in the way.

"And who do we have here?" Lawrence turned his hypnotic smile to Sloane.

"Excuse me for being so rude." Alice-Miranda grabbed Sloane and brought her closer to the group.

"This is Sloane Sykes. Sloane, this is my aunt Charlotte and soon-to-be uncle, Lawrence Ridley."

"How do you do, Miss Sykes?" Lawrence bowed his head.

"It's lovely to meet you, Sloane." Charlotte nodded.

"Gosh, you're gorgeous!" Sloane had clearly fallen for Lawrence's charm. "I mean, it's a pleasure to meet you too, Lawrence."

Sloane ignored Charlotte altogether as she stood mesmerized by the movie star.

"You're just in time for afternoon tea," Alice-Miranda informed them. "Mrs. Smith was so excited when I told her that you were coming, I think she's cooked enough to feed a small army."

The group headed for the dining room. Sunday afternoons were often quiet, as girls were out and about, enjoying their weekend freedom. Yet this afternoon the room was packed, and even the teachers had turned up.

"Did you tell everyone they were coming?" Jacinta hissed at Sloane.

"No," she replied innocently. "Why would I do that?"

Jacinta shook her head and Millie's face crumpled into a frown. The appearance of Lawrence caused a near riot. Girls were shouting out, asking him to come and sit with them. It was only when Miss Grimm took to the microphone that things settled down.

"Girls, please be quiet." Her ice-cold stare had the desired effect. "We have visitors for afternoon tea and yes, one of them is a wee bit famous and the other is an Old Girl of the school. However, that is no reason for the sort of behavior I have just witnessed. Mr. Ridley and Miss Highton-Smith are here as guests. Please do not pester them or ask for autographs. As your headmistress, I promise I will get an autograph which will suffice for all." Ophelia smiled.

The hush that had fallen over the room was maintained as Miss Grimm invited Lawrence and Charlotte to find a seat. She then hurried over and produced what appeared to be a rolled-up poster for Lawrence's latest movie, *London Calling,* and a thick black marker, which she handed to Lawrence. He signed the poster and, when Mr. Grump appeared with a camera, Lawrence posed for several photographs with the headmistress.

Miss Grimm chatted with Lawrence and Charlotte for what seemed like ages. Finally, Alice-Miranda interrupted them and asked if anyone would like tea.

"Oh, I am sorry, Alice-Miranda." Ophelia blushed. "I know your aunt and uncle have come to see you. I'll be off now."

"You have to try some of this cake." Millie pushed a piece of passion-fruit sponge toward Charlotte.

"So, how is Lucas?" Jacinta asked.

"Yes, how did he seem when you left him at school?" Alice-Miranda quizzed. "You know, we're doing a play with Fayle, and the rehearsals and everything will be over in their new drama theater. We've all tried out, so hopefully we'll be able to see Lucas a lot."

"He was okay." Lawrence nodded. "When I went to Fayle, it was a great school—never had any problems with bullies or the like. And his roommate is a really impressive young man."

"What's his name?" Sloane asked.

"Sep," Charlotte replied.

Sloane almost choked on her tea.

"Sep, as in Septimus, as in my brother, Septimus Sykes?" she babbled. "My brother is sharing a room with your son?!"

"Oh, that's great." Lawrence smiled *that* smile. Half the girls in the room almost fainted.

"Isn't that lovely?" Alice-Miranda grinned.

Jacinta wasn't so sure. She hoped that Septimus Sykes wasn't at all like his sister. Otherwise Lawrence's recollections about bullies at Fayle might prove nothing more than a long-distant memory.

Chapter 25

Sloane Sykes stalked off to telephone her mother. She was furious. Anyone would have thought Alice-Miranda was the movie star, the way the girls had all mobbed her after her aunt and Lawrence Ridley had left. Just watching the whole display turned Sloane's stomach. Life simply wasn't fair. Why couldn't her mother have married someone like Lawrence Ridley instead of her loser vacuum-cleaner salesman father? Sloane dreaded the other girls finding out about that. She'd never live it down. At least she had proof of her mother's having been a successful model, even if it was a hundred years ago.

"Hello, Mummy," Sloane said.

"Are you having a good time?" her mother asked.

"No, not especially."

"You just need to make some friends, that's all," her mother cooed. September was enjoying her new-found freedom with her children away. It was lovely not having to do the daily school run—now she could loll about in bed until nine a.m. and spend the rest of the day pleasing herself. The last thing she wanted was for Sloane to come home again.

"Septimus has got a new roommate," Sloane drawled.

"That's nice. I'm glad you're keeping in touch with your brother. I was worried he wouldn't make any friends, being the strange little fellow that he is," said September, admiring her French manicure.

Sloane offered the smallest titbit of information. "His father's a movie star."

September dropped the phone. There was a rustling sound as she fumbled about, retrieving it from the floor. "What did you say?"

Sloane repeated herself, slowly. "Septimus's new roommate's father is a movie star."

"Oh my gosh, are you kidding?" Her mother steadied herself on the counter, then had to sit down.

"No, Mummy, I'm not kidding," Sloane said.

"Well, who is it, then?" September demanded.

"Some kid called Lucas," Sloane teased.

"I don't care about him," September spat. "Who's his father? Who's this movie star?"

"Umm, well, I just met him a little while ago," Sloane continued.

"Sloane Sykes, hurry up and tell me. Or do I have to drive over there and drag it out of you?" her mother demanded.

"Oh, it's Lawrence Ridley," Sloane sighed.

There was a dull thud at the other end of the line. September had fallen off the chair and was now picking herself up from the kitchen floor. Sloane could hear her mother's squeals and wondered if perhaps she was having a heart attack.

"Are you there, Mummy?" she asked. "Mummy, are you there?"

There was the sound of deep breathing—more like huffing and blowing—until September finally gathered herself together enough to speak. "Sloane Sykes, you'd better not be putting me on."

"I'm not, Mummy. He was just here a little while ago, having tea."

"Then why didn't you call me? I could have been there in an hour. You just don't think, do you, Sloane? And now I've missed my chance to meet Lawrence Ridley." There was another thud. Sloane rolled her eyes. She waited for her mother to come back on the line.

"Mother, I have to go."

"No, no, you don't. Tell me about him." September gathered herself together. "What's he like?"

"He's handsome and charming and he's marrying Alice-Miranda's aunt," Sloane grouched.

"Really? What's she like?" September asked. "Is she pretty?"

"She's okay, I suppose. But totally wrong for him." Sloane scratched at her pinkie nail.

"Not glamorous enough, it happens all the time. Movie stars always marry beneath them." Her mother clicked her tongue. "He needs someone more like . . . well, like me, I suppose."

"That's what I thought," Sloane replied. "But I have to go, Mummy." Sloane glanced up at the line of girls who were waiting to use the telephone. Mrs. Howard had appeared and was tapping her watch and giving Sloane very dark looks, before bustling out of the room with an armful of towels.

"Call me tomorrow," her mother demanded. "Is he coming back again soon?"

"Who?" Sloane asked.

"Lawrence Ridley, of course." September wondered where her daughter got her brain sometimes.

"I don't know," Sloane replied.

"Well, you'd better find out. Maybe we'll get invited to the wedding," September squealed.

"Yeah, maybe, if he goes through with it." Sloane turned her back to the line of girls waiting for the phone.

"Bye, darling." September hung up.

Sloane continued talking into the phone for at least another three minutes before she finally put it down.

"Sorry, girls, important business." She smiled like a toad in a swarm of flies.

"Sloane Sykes." Mrs. Howard reappeared. "In here, young lady. NOW!"

Sloane huffed and walked to Mrs. Howard's little office, which was across the hallway from the sitting room.

"Close the door," Mrs. Howard commanded.

The girls waiting to use the phone listened intently as Sloane got a very solid telling off for being so inconsiderate of others.

Chapter 26

On Wednesday morning, just as Miss Reedy had promised, the cast list for the play was posted to the noticeboard outside the Great Hall. As morning tea finished, the girls spilled out of the dining room to check if they had secured a role.

"Alice-Miranda's Snow White," Millie squealed and hugged her little friend. "And Jacinta—you got the narrator." Jacinta breathed a sigh of relief. A group of taller girls had pushed in close. Millie was standing on tiptoe but had no chance of viewing the board.

"Millie, what are you?" Alice-Miranda asked.

Danika turned around and grinned at the smaller girls. "Millie's the Magic Mirror."

"That's great." Alice-Miranda smiled and squeezed Millie's hand.

Sloane was standing back from the group.

Jacinta turned to her roommate. "What about you, Sloane?"

"I'm in no hurry," she sneered. "Seriously, who else could play the Queen like me?"

Jacinta muttered under her breath, "You've got that right."

"What was that?" Sloane glared.

"Um, nothing, I just said yes, it's a part with real bite." Jacinta blinked innocently.

Ashima and Susannah linked arms. "Hi ho, hi ho, it's off to class we go," they sang, thrilled with their parts as Dopey and Doc.

Ivory was excited to be named head of the stage crew, and Danika was in the group working on costume design.

"I wonder who my Prince will be?" Alice-Miranda thought out loud.

"It says here Sep Sykes." Shelby turned around from the board, disappointed that she'd missed out on being one of the dwarfs, but consoled by her role as the lead tree in the forest.

"That's great." Alice-Miranda smiled. "Did you hear that, Sloane? Your brother is playing the Prince!"

"How lovely for you," Sloane drawled.

The taller girls dispersed, leaving Sloane, Alice-Miranda and Millie to check through the complete list. Sloane moved forward and ran her finger down the page.

"Told you so," she said aloud. "Evil Queen—Sloane Sykes."

"I guess it won't be a stretch just playing yourself," Millie quipped.

"Millie, that wasn't very kind," Alice-Miranda reprimanded her friend.

"Sorry," Millie apologized. "It's just that I couldn't imagine you having a more suitable part either, Sloane."

"Look!" Alice-Miranda gasped. "It says that the Woodcutter is Lucas Nixon. I'm so glad he arrived in time to audition."

"Good for him." Millie smiled. "There's no better way to fit in at school than to get involved. . . ."

Sloane rolled her eyes at Millie.

"Well, that's what Miss Reedy's always saying." Millie pulled a face back at her.

The first read-through with the cast was to take place the following afternoon. The girls were to meet Miss Reedy and walk with her to the other side of the village to Fayle, where all of the rehearsals would take place. The school had recently built a state-of-the-art drama facility, which would be perfect for the play.

"We'd better get to class." Alice-Miranda said goodbye to Millie and Jacinta and strode off to science with Mr. Plumpton. She always looked forward to his lessons, as they usually involved some type of experiment—which rarely went according to plan.

"Shall we go riding after school?" she called to Millie.

"That would be great." Millie winked. "Meet you at the stables at half past three."

Chapter 27

"**S**o where are you two going this fine afternoon?" Wally Whitstable was sitting in the middle of the stables on a bale of straw, oiling an old saddle.

"Hello, Wally." Alice-Miranda smiled. "We're just going for a loop over to Gertrude's Grove and home again."

She placed a small backpack outside Bonaparte's stall. Mrs. Smith had happily handed over three large slices of hummingbird cake and three chocolate brownies when Alice-Miranda had earlier appeared at the kitchen door. She explained that they were going out riding and wouldn't be around for tea.

"That's quite a long way, girls. Make sure you're back before dark. That forest gets awful creepy once the light fades," Wally warned.

"We'll be fine," Millie said as she grabbed Chops's bridle from the tack room wall.

"Watch that bloke of yours today, miss." Wally pointed at Bonaparte's stable. "I was giving 'im a nice rubdown before and the little monster nipped me on the ear. Drew blood, he did."

"Bonaparte." Alice-Miranda shook her head. "I just don't understand your lack of manners. You've grown up with some of the best-tempered horses I've ever met and still you behave like a spoilt little boy. I am sorry, Wally. One day he might learn to behave, but I am afraid I have my doubts." Bonaparte looked at his mistress with the sad eyes of a child in trouble.

"I haven't seen Miss Sloane down here again." Wally grinned. "I think Stumps might have put paid to her riding career."

"She says that she's waiting for her horse to arrive. Do you remember what she said his name was?" Millie asked.

"Yes, didn't she call him Harry?" Wally replied.

"That's what I thought. Then, the other day, she said that she was waiting for Hugo. I think her horse might be a figment of her overactive imagination." Millie pursed her lips.

"Don't be too hard on her, Millie," Alice-Miranda said. "Maybe she really wants a horse but her parents can't afford one. It costs a lot of money to come to a school like this, and ponies are very expensive."

"But her mother's a model and her dad's on television—or so I heard." Millie lifted her saddle down from the post on the wall and walked over to where she had Chops tied up in the stable.

"Television did you say, Miss Millie? What's Miss Sloane's surname, then?" Wally asked.

"Sykes, she's Sloane Sykes," Millie replied.

"That name does ring a bell." Wally stopped polishing the leather and tapped his lip thoughtfully. "I know. There's a bloke on the 'ome shopping channel called Smedley Sykes. My old nan's always got that on. She thinks he's a bit of a looker."

"There you are, then. That could be him," said Alice-Miranda as she led Bonaparte out of the stall, his shoes clip-clopping on the cobbled floor.

"But what does he *do* on the home shopping channel?" Millie asked.

"I think he sells gym equipment." Wally poured some more polish onto the cleaning cloth. "No, that's some other bloke Nan likes looking at too. Hang about. It's, um—oh, that's it. He sells vacuum cleaners. They're beauties too. I bought one for Nan last year for Christmas and she loves it. She sucked Uncle Alf's rug right off the top of his bald head one day when he wouldn't lift his feet off the carpet."

Millie roared with laughter, imagining Wally's uncle losing his toupee up the vacuum cleaner.

"Well, Mr. Sykes isn't exactly the television star that Sloane would want everyone to believe." Millie giggled.

"I don't think Sloane ever mentioned that he *was* on television. Didn't one of the other girls say that? I think it was Ashima who said that she overheard Mrs. Howard talking to Mrs. Derby about Sloane's parents," Alice-Miranda replied as she pulled up a stool and hauled herself onto Bonaparte's back.

"Maybe," Millie said. "She's probably embarrassed. I'd die if my father was on the television lifting bowling balls with a vacuum."

"No, you wouldn't," Alice-Miranda said. "There's nothing wrong with being in sales. I mean, look at my mummy and daddy. Our family livelihood depends on department stores and supermarkets."

Chops and Bonaparte were ready to go.

"Take care there, girls. See you soon." Wally stood up and gave Bonaparte a friendly pat. The pony repaid his kindness by trying to bite his finger. "Off with you then, you little monster."

Alice-Miranda and Millie trotted to the gate. Once on the other side, they cantered across the field and into the woods toward Caledonia Manor. Just as they had done on Sunday, the girls left the ponies in the stall outside the stables. Alice-Miranda led the way as they raced up the driveway to the house.

"Hello, Miss Hephzibah," Alice-Miranda called as she knocked, then walked straight into the kitchen with Millie behind her. "We're here, and we've brought cake and brownies too."

The old woman emerged from the playroom and Alice-Miranda ran to give her a hug. Hephzibah didn't know how to respond, having lived for such a long time without human affection. She gently patted the child on the back. Millie was more cautious, saying hello from where she stood.

"Hello." Hephzibah nodded. "Please come." Her left palm was outstretched, indicating that they would sit at the pine table in the middle of the kitchen. There were three cups and saucers with matching plates out ready. "It's good to see you again . . . so soon. I . . . I wasn't sure that you would come. . . ." Her voice faltered.

"Of course we were going to come and see you." Alice-Miranda unpacked the contents of the backpack and busied herself distributing Mrs. Smith's sweet treats. "But I'm afraid we can't stay for too long or Wally will send a search party."

Hephzibah was dressed in the same black clothes with her hat and veil shielding her scarred face. When Alice-Miranda had visited last time with Millie, the old woman had not removed either and had kept her face hidden. Hephzibah had seen in Millie the fear of a child who had been told the witch stories, and she was anxious not to cause further alarm. There was something lovely about Millie's red hair and sprinkling of freckles like paprika that reminded Hephzibah of someone long ago. Someone she had loved with all her heart.

The trio sat down to their afternoon tea party.

"We're doing a play with the boys at Fayle," Alice-Miranda began. "Millie's going to play the part of the Magic Mirror."

"And Alice-Miranda's Snow White," Millie added.

Hephzibah looked up at the girls with a flicker of a smile hiding on her lips.

"A play, how wonderful. When I was a girl, I played

{173}

the part of Snow White too," she spoke softly. "It was marvelous."

"That's amazing!" Alice-Miranda gasped. "You can help me learn my lines." The tiny child beamed.

Hephzibah clasped her bony hands in front of her. "That was a million years ago—another lifetime. I was a different person then."

"But it will be fun," Alice-Miranda insisted. "Anyway, next time we come, we can bring our scripts, can't we Millie?"

Millie took a bite of chocolate brownie and nodded.

Alice-Miranda sipped her tea. She placed her cup back on the saucer, and for a moment, there was complete silence among the three of them.

"Have you always lived here?" Alice-Miranda asked.

Hephzibah rested her cake fork on the side of her plate. Something about this tiny child with her cascading chocolate curls and eyes as big as saucers made her feel safe.

"Yes," Hephzibah replied. "Would you like to have a look around?"

"Yes, please." Alice-Miranda stood up. "That would be wonderful."

Chapter 28

September Sykes sat on the couch watching her favorite television game show, *Winners Are Grinners*. A painful memory invaded her thoughts. Smedley had auditioned to be the host of that show fifteen years ago. He made it to the final two and then Cody Taylor, who she was now watching on the television, was given the job.

At the time, September had begged Smedley to change his name. She'd been keen on Saxon, but he wouldn't hear of it. Cody Taylor was now one of the most sought-after presenters in the country. He owned an island and fourteen sports cars and his real name was Wilfred Thicke.

Life simply isn't fair, September thought. At least things were changing for the better.

For a start, September was thrilled that Septimus was rooming with the son of the most handsome movie star on the planet. And if she wasn't free to marry Lawrence Ridley herself, at least she could get herself and Smedley invited to Lawrence's star-studded celebrity wedding. She could imagine what the girls at the gym would say about that. And then there was Smedley's new business. He'd used the proceeds from the sale of his father's shop to buy into a company building condominiums for cashed-up retirees chasing the sun overseas. He'd shown her the brochures—the apartments were gorgeous, and the whole scheme was certain to turn a handsome profit. The kids were tucked away at boarding school, and September simply didn't have a minute to miss them. Life was certainly on the way up.

The last contestant had just blown it. "Oh, you silly cow," September shouted at the television. "Everyone knows that it's God who's richer than the Queen." She pressed the Off button on the remote before seeing the answer, which actually named a famous children's author as the correct response.

September picked up the phone and dialed the common room at Fayle.

"Hello," she purred. It's September, Septimus's mother."

"Oh, hello, Mrs. Sykes," the house master, Mr. Huntley, replied.

"Please, call me September." She smiled down the phone. "Is my darling Septimus about?"

"I'm sorry, Mrs. Sy—I mean, September, but Sep is, er, at . . ." He ran his finger down the list of names on the sheet which gave him the whereabouts of all the boys at their afternoon activities. "Your son is currently at football training."

"Football? That doesn't sound like Sep at all," September replied.

"Well, I can assure you that's where he is. Would you like me to have him phone you when he gets in?" Mr. Huntley inquired.

"Yes, I've called four times now since the weekend, but he's never available," September moaned. "Anyone would think he loves that school more than his own mother."

"No, I'm sure that's not true at all. Sep is doing a great job of settling in. I don't remember a boy so enthusiastic about being involved in . . . well, just about everything. There's nothing to worry about." Horatio Huntley was losing his patience and thanking his lucky stars that it must have been one of the other residents who had taken Mrs. Sykes's calls on the previous three occasions.

"Well, I haven't got time to keep phoning, Mr. Hunter," September tutted.

"It's Huntley, Horatio Huntley, madam," he corrected her.

"Whatever. Perhaps you can tell me about his new little roommate?"

"Yes, of course. He's a good lad, name's Lucas Nixon. I think they're getting along extremely well. Both keen on their sports and their studies, and they've both won themselves parts in the school play that we're doing with the girls from Winchesterfield-Downsfordvale," Mr. Huntley offered.

"So he's an actor, just like his father." September grinned and checked her reflection in the refrigerator door.

Horatio sighed. "I'm sorry, September, but I'm not at liberty to discuss the boy's family."

"Well, of course you can, Horatio," September assured him. "You know I won't tell anyone—and he is sharing a room with my son. I'd like to know that his parents are good eggs. Don't want to find out darling Sep is sleeping next to the son of an axe murderer or something."

Horatio had just about had enough. "Mrs. Sykes,

I'm terribly sorry, but I must go. One of the boys has just superglued his finger to his science project. I'll let Sep know you called." And with that, he hung up.

"Rude," September huffed.

Smedley arrived home just as the call finished. His brow looked like ten rows of pearl-stitch knitting and he was as pale as a pint of milk.

"You have to call the headmaster at Fayle, Smedley, and make a complaint about that rude house master, Mr. Huntley." September opened the fridge and retrieved two large prepacked tubs of potato salad. "He just hung up on me."

"Really?" Smedley looked at his wife. "Why?"

"Some stupid brat had superglued his finger to his science project or something. Surely he could have waited."

September took the lids off the plastic tubs and emptied their contents onto two plates.

"Oh, we're not back on that again, are we?" Smedley screwed up his face. "A man can't live on potato salad alone. Can't we have some meat?"

"No. I've just started the carbo-salad diet, and if I have to suffer, you do too." September pushed the plate in front of her husband.

Smedley glanced at the pile of letters on the countertop and sighed loudly.

"I have to go out," he gulped.

"Why?" September demanded.

"Business." He grabbed his briefcase and jammed the letters inside.

She pouted. "When will you be back, then?"

"Later." Smedley strode out the back door.

September heard the car door slam and the tires squeal as he backed out of the driveway. As she sat at the kitchen table picking her way through the potato salad, she noticed a letter that must have fallen on the floor when Smedley grabbed the pile off the countertop.

She reached down to get it and noticed the words *Private and Confidential* emblazoned across the top. Her stomach did a backflip. "What's all this, then?"

September marched over and flicked the switch to start the kettle.

Chapter 29

Alice-Miranda bounced along beside Miss
Reedy all the way to Fayle. The steel-gray sky
was threatening rain, but Miss Reedy armed the
girls with their raincoats and umbrellas, knowing
that a brisk walk was just the thing to get them settled before the first read-through of the play. The
group marched in two straight lines through the
tiny village of Winchesterfield: past the Victorian
terraces, past the butcher, baker and post office
and past the little grocery shop with the flat
above, which used to belong to Sloane Sykes's grandfather Percy. The longest part of the walk was
down the hedge-lined driveway at Winchesterfield-

Downsfordvale and back up the even longer driveway at Fayle.

"What a lovely school," Alice-Miranda remarked as they walked along a pathway bordered on both sides by clipped camellia hedges. On the way over, Miss Reedy and her smallest charge had chatted about all manner of things—books they'd read, Miss Reedy's recent trip to the city and ideas for some of the scenes in the play. Miss Reedy had written the adaptation herself and was keen to see it come together. When at last the main school building came into view, Alice-Miranda couldn't help feeling as if she'd been there before.

Millie caught up to her friend. She'd spent the walk chatting to Jacinta. Only a few months ago, the two barely spoke at all, but since Alice-Miranda had arrived at school, Millie had come to realize that although Jacinta was a little highly strung, she was really very good fun.

"It's huge, isn't it?" Millie looked up at the building, with its four Ionic columns and grand portico. Then she thought for a moment. "You know what this place looks like?" She tilted her head to one side.

Alice-Miranda nodded. "Yes. That's it. It's almost exactly the same."

"The same as what?" Miss Reedy asked, glancing down at the tiny girls.

"Oh, the same as a friend's house." Alice-Miranda smiled.

"Goodness, you do have fortunate friends to live in a house like this. It's beautiful, isn't it?" Miss Reedy admired the detailed plasterwork.

One half of the double front doors swung open and Mr. Lipp emerged. His red suit stood out against the dreary day.

"Good afternoon, ladies." He nodded. "We'll head straight to the drama center. The boys are gathering there now."

Millie and Alice-Miranda fell to the rear of the group as they took in every detail of the mansion. A shiny brass nameplate beside the front doors bore the building's name: MCGLINTOCK MANOR.

"Come along, girls," Mr. Lipp called as he waited for the group at a stone archway. "We must get started posthaste."

Alice-Miranda and Millie ran to catch up.

The drama center, though apparently brand-new, looked as if it had been part of the school forever. The girls were ushered through an opulent foyer and into the top of a large theater with curved rows of tiered seating and a stage area below. They walked in single file down to the bottom two rows. The girls were directed to take a seat on the left-hand side, while the boys from Fayle sat on the far right. Jacinta spotted Lucas first of all. She waved frantically. He looked up and raised his left hand.

"Which one is your brother?" Alice-Miranda asked Sloane, who had sat down beside her.

Sloane gazed over at the group of twenty or so boys. "There he is." Sloane shuddered. "Next to that boy waving."

"Oh, that's Lucas. They must be friends already." Alice-Miranda stood up and waved to her soon-to-be cousin. "He looks just like his dad, doesn't he?"

Sloane peered across at the boys and nodded. He certainly did.

"Jacinta adores him," Alice-Miranda stated. "I do too, but not in *that* way. They didn't like each other at all a few weeks ago, but then they had a long chat and voila, they became great friends."

Sloane decided right there and then what she must do. Jacinta was no match for her charms. If Sloane played her cards right, Lucas would be falling all over her in no time.

Mr. Lipp and Miss Reedy stood side by side on the stage, looking up at the assembled students. It was

{184}

Miss Reedy who spoke first, about the importance of learning lines and being on time for rehearsals. Her stern voice rang out through the theater, apparently coming as quite a shock to some of the boys, whose faces took on a pale tinge.

Her message was loud and clear. "Tardiness will *not* be tolerated, inappropriate behavior of any sort will *not* be tolerated and missing rehearsals for any reason other than extreme illness will *not* be tolerated. This is the first time that our two schools have joined forces in over ten years. I would like this to become an annual tradition once more, as would you, Mr. Lipp, I presume." She frowned at the teacher beside her, who nodded like a jack-in-the-box. "As we enter a new age of cooperation, I look forward to nothing less than a performance of the highest standard. And, above all"—her voice softened—"I hope that you will have a lot of fun in the process."

"Fun? Is she kidding?" Lucas whispered behind his hand to Sep. "She's terrifying. Glad she doesn't work here."

"What was that, young man?" Miss Reedy glared up at Lucas.

"Nothing, miss. I was just saying I can't wait to get started," he lied.

Sep had not taken his eyes off Miss Reedy, who

apparently had a built-in tracking and radar system capable of picking up even the softest of sounds and most minuscule movements. He thought she'd be a valuable asset to the government's security agency with those skills.

Mr. Lipp then handed out the scripts. Each student's name was printed clearly at the top and their lines had been highlighted throughout.

"Oh, and please don't lose those," Miss Reedy added, "or you will be writing them out again by hand."

There was an audible gulp from the group.

The read-through began. Several of the students decided to try out different accents, with varying degrees of success. One young lad, playing the role of Sneezy, sounded like a breathless old man and was told under no circumstances could he keep that voice, until Mr. Lipp pointed out to Miss Reedy that it was, in fact, his real voice. The poor lad was suffering terribly with allergies, which Mr. Lipp thought added to the authenticity of the part.

An hour passed, and Miss Reedy and Mr. Lipp seemed pleased with the students' efforts. They indicated that the children could head up to the foyer for a few minutes while the teachers conferred on some matters.

The girls and boys left the theater. They walked up

opposite aisles and milled about in two separate groups, until Alice-Miranda marched over to say hello to Lucas.

"There you are." She smiled. "How are you getting on?"

Lucas nodded. "Fine. Yeah, it's good."

"Jacinta, Millie," Alice-Miranda called. "Come and say hello."

The two girls walked over to join the pair. Jacinta was just about to say something, when Sloane Sykes appeared.

"Hello," she purred. "You must be Lucas. I feel soooo sorry for you."

"Why?" Lucas replied.

"You have to share a room with my disgusting brother." She grimaced.

"Oh, so you're Sloane," said Lucas.

"Yes." She fluttered her eyelashes.

"There's no need to feel sorry for me. Sep and I are getting on great." He grinned—and there it was, that million-dollar smile, just like his father's.

Sloane smiled back. "I met your dad the other day."

"Yeah, me too." Lucas smirked. Alice-Miranda, Jacinta and Millie giggled. Sloane laughed too, though she had no idea what she was laughing about.

"Next time we come over to Fayle, you'll have to show us around," Jacinta said.

"Yeah, that'd be great. Although there are heaps of places I don't know yet either," Lucas replied.

Septimus Sykes was standing on the other side of the room, hoping to avoid his sister. She was bound to make a scene. Lucas spotted him and motioned to his friend to join them. Sep didn't move.

"Hang on a minute," Lucas told the girls, and waved again at Sep. Septimus was reluctant, but he didn't want to disappoint Lucas and seem rude. He walked over to his friend.

"Hello." Alice-Miranda held out her tiny hand. "My name is Alice-Miranda Highton-Smith-Kennington-Jones and I'm very pleased to meet you, Sep."

Septimus couldn't help but smile.

"These are my friends, Millie and Jacinta." She nodded at the girls. "And I think you know Sloane."

Millie and Jacinta smiled, but Sloane just curled her lip into a snarl.

"Hello," Septimus said to Millie and Jacinta. He glanced at his sister. "I see you're in a good mood, as usual."

"All the better for seeing you, big brother," Sloane bit back.

Miss Reedy and Mr. Plumpton appeared in the foyer.

"Come along, girls, we must be going," Miss Reedy boomed. "You'll need to put your raincoats on."

"See you soon." Alice-Miranda gave Lucas a quick hug. His face turned the color of Mr. Lipp's suit.

With the exception of Sloane, the other children exchanged polite goodbyes. "Bye . . . see you tomorrow . . . nice to meet you . . ."

Miss Reedy stood tall at the head of the line. Outside, it had started to drizzle.

"It's so cold," Sloane grouched. "I don't know why we couldn't have taken the bus."

"Moral fortitude, young lady." Miss Reedy's bionic hearing had kicked in again. "Stop complaining or we'll go the long way around." The teacher glanced at Alice-Miranda beside her and winked.

Alice-Miranda giggled as they set off through the damp air for home.

Chapter 30

September Sykes was seething. She had just arrived home from her daily workout at the gym and checked the phone messages. She had hoped to hear from Septimus but instead, Golden Gates had left four messages asking her if she could get in touch to organize the return of her stepmother-in-law's suitcase.

"What's in that thing?" she grouched. "Gold bars?"

Things were not going as planned in the Sykes household. Steaming open her husband's private and confidential letter had sent Sloane into an incandescent rage. It seemed that Smedley's "can't lose, license to print money" retirement-villa scheme was already in trouble. Apparently the construction company had hit a sewer line the previous week when drilling the foundations, spilling thousands of liters of raw sewage into the street and flooding several houses. The cleanup was going to cost thousands and the insurance company refused to cover it. She had confronted Smedley when he arrived home, but he simply told her that it was all going to be just fine and he'd already sorted it out. She didn't believe him.

September had a shower and changed into her favorite pink leisure suit. She made herself a cup of coffee using the shiny silver machine Smedley had given her for Christmas, opened a packet of choc-chip biscuits and pranced out to the back garden to soak up the sun. She needed something to take her mind off her stupid husband and his dodgy business deals. She remembered that she'd left the latest copy of *Gloss and Goss* on top of her gym towel on a pile of laundry. She jumped up to get it and stubbed her toe on the battered blue suitcase Smedley had left beside the utility room door.

"Oh, blast and blast," she yelled. "My toe!" Plump tears wobbled, then spilled down September's perfectly made-up cheeks. "Smedley, you idiot!" she yelled. At that moment, the telephone rang. September hopped inside on one leg to pick it up.

"Hello," she said, wincing.

"Oh, hello, Mrs. Sykes, is it?"

"Yes," September grouched.

"It's Matron Payne from Golden Gates. I am terribly glad to find you at home. I've been calling and calling and I wasn't sure if you'd received any of my messages."

"What do you want, then?" September rubbed her big toe.

"Well, Mrs. Sykes, it's your mother-in-law," Matron Payne began.

"She's my stepmother-in-law."

"Of course, your stepmother-in-law." Matron Payne was not enjoying September's tone at all.

"Has she died?" September asked.

"No, she's as well as can be expected under the circumstances." It was fortunate September couldn't see the matron, who was quivering in disgust.

"What is it, then? I'm very busy. I don't have all day." September was thinking about her coffee getting cold.

"Your stepmother-in-law has been asking about a blue suitcase. Apparently it's very important to her.

As you know, she hasn't been able to speak since the stroke and her writing is awfully wobbly, but this morning she spent rather a long time creating a message which indicated that she is fretting terribly for it. The doctor says it would most likely help speed her recovery if it were found and returned to her immediately," Matron Payne explained.

"I have no idea what you're talking about." September walked to the patio doors and looked directly at the suitcase, which she had just tripped over.

"Well, Mrs. Sykes, could you please have a look for it? I know your stepmother-in-law would be very grateful." Matron Payne was fast losing patience.

"I'll tell my husband and he can bring it round, if he finds it, that is. I have to go." September hung up.

"Mrs. Sykes," Matron Payne began, then realized that the line was dead. "I'm sure your stepmother-in-law, Henrietta, one of the loveliest ladies I've ever had the pleasure to care for, would be happy to have some visitors," she whispered into the beeping handset.

September had already decided midway through the conversation that the battered blue suitcase must contain something of value. Why else would the old girl be so desperate to have it back? She dragged the case toward the outdoor setting and lifted it onto the table. A rusty padlock guarded its contents. September went to the shed and found a pair of pliers with which she mangled the lock until it snapped in two. It was only tiny and came away quite easily. As she unzipped the case and pushed open the flap, a smell of mildew, moldy socks and Stilton cheese rose up and hit her in the nostrils.

"Pooh!" September held her nose and waved her hand. "So where's the treasure?"

At first glance, it seemed that the contents were nothing more than a pile of old papers. There were some photographs and faded newspaper clippings, but no gold bars or bags of diamonds. September continued rummaging and found an antique pipe and a framed photograph of a man from long ago.

"What a lot of sentimental rubbish," she said out loud. She was about to close the lid when something caught her eye. It was a piece of yellowed parchment written in fancy lettering. The name at the top was familiar. *Fayle*. She pulled it from the pile and laid it on the table. It was a family tree; the bottom left-hand corner was missing and there were some holes in the page, but it was unmistakable. It was the Fayle family tree. September wondered if it had anything to do with the school.

"Here it is." She followed the trail with her finger.

"Frederick Erasmus Fayle, founder of Fayle School for Boys, married Helena Louise McGlintock. They had one son and they lived at McGlintock Manor, which it says here is the schoolhouse. George Mc-Glintock Fayle married Edwina Elena Rochester. They had one son called Erasmus McGlintock Fayle. Gawd, what a terrible name! They lived at the schoolhouse too. Then Erasmus married someone called Willow Caledonia Henry and they had—Well, of course, this part's missing, isn't it? *D-A-U-G-H*—it must have been a daughter. Here it is, then. Henrietta McGlintock Fayle. *Our Henrietta?*" September screwed up her nose. "Granny Henrietta was a Fayle?"

September wondered what else she might learn about her stepmother-in-law. All this time and the old duck had never said anything. September was sure her name was Henrietta McGlintock, but she'd never mentioned being a Fayle. And the only thing she'd ever paid for was the children's new school fees, which September now decided she likely got for free anyway, seeing as though she probably owned the school. September tutted and rolled her eyes. As she did so, she spotted another piece of paper in the case. She snatched it up and unfolded it. It looked much older than the first document and was also damaged at the bottom. She couldn't tell how much of it was missing. Again, she read aloud.

"'Fayle School Charter. This document outlines the rules by which Fayle School for Boys is herewith established. Number one: the school motto will henceforth be *Nomine defectus non autem natura—Fail by name, not by nature.*' That's a bit stupid, isn't it? 'Number two: boys will be trained in academic, artistic and athletic pursuits'—isn't that what all schools do?" September shook her head. "'Number three: only teachers of the highest caliber will be employed at the school. Number four: Fayle will remain on the site purchased by the school's founder, Frederick Erasmus Fayle, on one thousand acres of land in the village of Winchesterfield.' Boring—blah, blah, blah." September ran her finger down the remainder of the list. "What's this? . . . 'Number twenty-nine: failure at Fayle is not acceptable. Should more than twenty-five percent of boys fail ANY examination, the headmaster incumbent'—I wonder what that means—'must invoke clause thirty of the Fayle School Charter . . .' Well, what's that rule?" September scanned farther down. "Ah, here it is." She tapped her red talon on the page. "'The school must be closed within twenty-eight days and all land, buildings and other assets be returned to the oldest living relative of Frederick Erasmus Fayle.'"

September's eyes almost popped out of her head. She reread the paragraph. Then she reread the family tree. One child, that was all the Fayles ever had. One child in every generation. If this was true, then Smedley's stepmother would be the next in line to the Fayle family fortune. And she was old and sick, and probably wouldn't live for much longer.

"Oh, this is the answer to all our problems!" September folded the charter and family tree, stuffed the rest of the papers back into the suitcase and zipped it up. "I don't think we ever did find that bag," she said to herself as she dragged it into the house. "I think that bag must have gone missing somewhere." She stopped in the hallway and pulled down the attic ladder. Her mind was racing. A wicked plan was brewing, and she knew just the girl to help her with it.

Chapter 31

The girls arrived back at school in time for tea. Mrs. Smith had decided to expand her catering repertoire this term, with themed dinners once a week from countries around the world. Tonight she had whipped up butter chicken with rice, naan bread and a mild beef vindaloo curry. Dessert was a delicious sweet dumpling dish.

"What's this muck?" Sloane pushed her food around the bowl. "It's disgusting."

"Don't you like it?" Alice-Miranda asked. "I think it's scrumptious. Last year, when Mummy and Daddy took me to visit their friend, Prince Shivaji, I fell in love with Indian desserts. But I can tell you this *gulab jamun* is the best I've ever tasted. Mrs. Smith is so clever."

"She's certainly improved, that's for sure." Jacinta nodded. "You don't remember, but her food used to be awful."

"All that time with Mrs. Oliver must have improved her technique. Now, there's a great cook." Millie rubbed her tummy and shoveled another spoonful of the sticky treat into her mouth.

"Your brother's lovely, Sloane." Alice-Miranda set her spoon down inside the empty bowl.

"My brother's a pig," Sloane replied.

"I wish I had a brother," Alice-Miranda said. "But at least I'm getting a cousin."

"So, when's the wedding?" Sloane asked.

"I'm not sure. It will depend on Uncle Lawrence's film schedules and Aunt Charlotte's work too."

"Will there be lots of famous people there?" Sloane didn't want to sound desperate, but she simply had to get an invitation.

"I don't know, really. I mean, Aunt Charlotte and Uncle Lawrence have lots of friends, but I'm not sure if they're famous," Alice-Miranda said thoughtfully.

"Of course they'd be famous. Don't famous people only hang out with other famous people? I mean, look at your mother, Jacinta. She's always with

{199}

beautiful people doing important things in interesting places," Sloane informed the group.

"I don't really know what my mother does or who she's friends with." Jacinta's lip quivered. "And it's not really any of your business either."

"You're kidding, aren't you? Your mother is in every edition of *Women's Daily* and *Gloss and Goss* I've ever seen. She's practically their poster girl for famous people doing fun things with other famous people."

"I don't care." Jacinta glowered. "What my mother does is entirely up to her."

"If my mother was as famous as that, I'd talk to her every day and I'd tell everyone where she'd been and who she was with."

"Good, I'll tell her to adopt you. Perhaps we can trade mothers."

"Now you really are kidding, aren't you?" Millie laughed. Jacinta smiled too. That was a terrible thought.

"What's wrong with my mother?" Sloane fizzed with anger. "She's beautiful and she was a famous model too. What does your mother do, Millie?"

"Millie's mother is a vet," Alice-Miranda contributed. "And she's awfully good. You know, Chops had a mystery virus and he could have died, but Millie's mother solved the puzzle and cured him. And she started an animal shelter for unwanted pets."

"Wow," said Sloane sarcastically, rolling her eyes. "And what's your dad? A lion tamer?"

"He's a farmer," Millie replied.

"Double wow," Sloane drawled.

"Well, at least my father doesn't peddle vacuum cleaners on the home shopping channel for a living." Millie couldn't help herself. It was out of her mouth before she had time to think.

"Why, you little brat!" Sloane screamed, and stood up. She picked up her bowl of *gulab jamun,* marched around to where Millie was sitting and tipped the entire contents over her head.

Millie bellowed. She grabbed Sloane by her long blond ponytail and yanked as hard as she could.

"Ow, you brat!"

The chinking of cutlery died down as the other girls turned to see what was going on.

"Sloane Sykes, and Millicent Jane McLoughlin-McTavish-McNoughton-McGill, come here, NOW!" Miss Grimm bellowed across the room. Her general demeanor may have changed for the better, but she could still silence an entire dining room in a second.

Millie lifted the upended bowl from her head and set it back on the table. She turned to face her attacker, then marched toward the head table, where Miss Grimm stood with her arms folded in front of her. Sloane followed at a distance.

Miss Grimm lowered her voice and glared at the culprits. "*What* was that?"

"She started it." Sloane began to sob. "She said awful things about my mother and father."

"I did not," Millie retorted. "She's a bully, Miss Grimm."

"*Bully* is a very strong word, Millicent, and not one we throw around willy-nilly." Miss Grimm was inclined to believe her redheaded charge, but she had to keep an open mind. From where she and Miss Reedy were sitting, it did look as though Millicent had pulled Sloane's hair. But there was the indisputable evidence of the upended dessert. Millie was dripping dumplings onto the floor right in front of them.

Ophelia realized that the room was still silent. She looked up and addressed the girls. "Please go on with your dinner. Talk among yourselves. This is now a private matter and I will settle it with Millicent and Sloane. I will see both of you," she said, staring them down, "in my office, tomorrow morning at seven a.m. Do not be late, and remember, I *will* find out what happened, so it will be much easier if you tell me the truth. Off you go. You can sit at your table until the end of teatime."

Millicent glanced up at the clock on the wall. It was only a quarter past six. They didn't go back to the house until seven p.m. Her hair was beginning to set like concrete on the side of her face. She opened her mouth to speak.

"I would also suggest that you remain silent," Miss Grimm commanded.

Ophelia thought it was probably punishment enough that the girls had to stew on things for the night. She wasn't planning anything especially severe—perhaps some additional gardening duties with Charlie or mucking out the stables. She had a niggling feeling about Sloane Sykes, though, and after what had happened with Alethea Goldsworthy, she didn't plan on being fooled again.

Chapter 32

Back at the house, Millie sped straight for the showers to wash her hair. Sloane Sykes went straight for the telephone. She called her mother and immediately began to cry.

"Darling, what's the matter?" September fussed. "Why are you so upset?"

"I got into trouble with Miss Grimm. It wasn't my fault. Millie said mean things about you and Daddy," Sloane sobbed.

"Oh, sweetie, what did she say?"

Sloane began to wail even louder.

"Don't you worry your pretty head about that nasty little brat. I'm so glad you called, though. I have something important to tell you." Sloane's mother smiled. "Your father's not here, and that's a good thing, because this is a special secret just between you and me. Septimus doesn't need to know either, okay?"

"What is it, Mummy?" Sloane perked up.

"Did you know that if twenty-five percent of the boys at Fayle fail any test, the school has to close immediately?"

"Yes. Alice-Miranda told me that. She says everyone knows it. But the boys at Fayle don't fail, and so nobody's ever worried about that silly rule," Sloane replied. "Why do you ask?"

"Well, sweetie, do you know what would happen to all that lovely land and those gorgeous buildings if the boys failed and the school had to close?"

"Yes. It gets sold off or something." Sloane twisted a long strand of blond hair around her index finger.

"Well, yes and no. The school has to close immediately, but the land and the buildings go to the next living relative of the school's founder—some fellow called Frederick Erasmus Fayle." September was enjoying this.

"Big deal, Mummy. I don't see what any of this has to do with us. We're Sykeses, not Fayles."

"I see what you mean. But did you know what Granny Henrietta's surname was before she married Grandpa Percy?" September asked.

"No, Mummy. Why would I know that?"

"I don't suppose you would." The mother was toying with her daughter like a kitten with a string. "But I do."

"Mother, get to the point. I have to go and paint my toenails," Sloane snapped.

"Sloane, I have recently learned that your darling stepgranny was once known as Henrietta McGlintock Fayle. And guess what? She's an only child." September waited for Sloane to realize what she had just said.

Sloane was not impressed. "Yeah, so what, Mummy? Granny Henrietta gets the school if the boys fail—which they won't, because they don't."

"But what if they did?" September lowered her voice. "What if they failed and Granny passed away? Work it out, sweetheart."

Sloane pondered for a moment. "That would mean Fayle, and all those beautiful buildings, and all that lovely land would go to . . . oh . . . Daddy!" She cupped her hand to the telephone. "Oh my gosh, Mother, you're a genius!"

"Thank you, darling." Possibly for the first time in her life, September *felt* like a true genius.

"But, Mummy, the boys at Fayle don't fail—not ever," Sloane reminded her mother.

"Well, darling, you see, that's where you come in. . . ."

Chapter 33

Alice-Miranda sat up in bed. "Good morning, Millie." She looked over at her friend. "How are you feeling?" Alice-Miranda had set her alarm for six a.m. She was planning to use the extra time to practice her lines for the play.

"Terrible," Millie sighed. "I didn't sleep much at all. Miss Grimm's probably going to kick me out of the play."

"I don't think so," Alice-Miranda reassured her. "She's changed so much, remember, and I'm sure if you apologize to Sloane, Miss Grimm will accept that. Sloane *was* being a bit tricky."

"Yes, but I have to keep my temper under better control."

The two girls hopped out of bed. Millie didn't want to be a second late for her appointment with Miss Grimm.

"Good luck." Alice-Miranda gave Millie a quick hug. "Just tell Miss Grimm the truth—that's all you can do."

It was a quarter to seven when Millie departed for Miss Grimm's study. The corridors of Winchester-field Manor were particularly foreboding in the early-morning light. Millie glanced at the portraits of the former headmistresses with their stern looks. She felt like they were all frowning at her.

Mrs. Derby hadn't yet arrived for the day, but Miss Grimm had obviously opened the office door for the girls. There was no sign of Sloane, and come to think of it, Millie hadn't seen her back at the house. Surely she wasn't stupid enough to miss the meeting?

Millie sat in one of the chairs positioned outside Miss Grimm's study to wait until seven a.m. She watched the grandfather clock against the wall. *Tick . . . tick . . . tick . . .* The rhythm of the grand old timepiece was like a slow march. Every minute seemed like an hour. In an effort to take her mind off her impending doom, Millie stood up and walked over to have a look at Mrs. Derby's row of photographs perched on the marble mantelpiece. There was a lovely picture of her and Constable Derby on their wedding day and another of Millie and Alice-Miranda as flower girls. In fact, Mrs. Derby had involved all of the girls in her celebration, each wearing pretty dresses in a rainbow of colors with floral garlands in their hair. Millie's own red locks stood out like a beacon compared with the other girls.

Millie walked back over to the mahogany chair and sat down. According to the clock, it was two minutes to seven. At seven a.m. precisely, she would knock.

Ding dong dong ding, dong ding ding dong . . . The clock rang out its merry tune.

Millie waited until the last chime before she reached up to tap on the mahogany door.

"Come!" Miss Grimm's voice boomed from within. She was sitting at her desk but stood up and indicated that Millie should take a seat on the leather chesterfield sofa near the fire.

"Is Sloane with you?" Miss Grimm asked.

"No, Miss Grimm," Millie replied.

"Well, she'd want to hurry." Miss Grimm glanced at her watch and the clock on the wall opposite her desk.

Ophelia sat down in one of the wingbacked armchairs opposite Millie. "Millie, would you like to explain to me, please, what happened last night?"

"I'm sorry, Miss Grimm. My behavior was unacceptable. I didn't mean to pull Sloane's hair. It's just that when she poured the *gulab* over me, I couldn't control my temper." Millie stared at the Persian carpet on the floor in front of her, mesmerized by its intricate pattern.

"All right, well, you can apologize to Sloane—when she gets here," Miss Grimm advised. "You might like to tell me the events that led to Sloane depositing her dessert on your head."

"Yes, Miss Grimm. Sloane was talking about Jacinta's mother and saying that if she were her mother, she'd tell everyone how famous she was and who she was with. Jacinta was a bit upset because, well, she never really sees her mother very much. Then Jacinta made a joke and said that she could trade mothers with Sloane, and I said that she had to be kidding, and Jacinta and I laughed. Sloane got angry and asked why we were laughing."

"And why were you laughing?" Miss Grimm asked. Her mouth was drawn into a tight line.

"Well, I suppose we thought it would be even worse having Sloane's mother," Millie admitted.

"And why do you think that?" Miss Grimm asked.

"I don't know exactly. It's just that Sloane's mother seems awfully caught up with who people know and what they look like. I suppose we laughed because we all know Jacinta's mother isn't exactly in the running for mother of the year, and the idea of her swapping her mother for Sloane's was really silly."

"Indeed." Miss Grimm drummed her fingers on the arm of the chair. She couldn't agree with Millie more, but it wasn't appropriate for her to say so. She caught Millie looking up at her sheepishly. "Was there anything else?" Miss Grimm asked.

"Yes. Sloane made fun of my mother when Alice-Miranda said she was a vet, and then she asked if my father was a lion tamer, and that's when I blurted out that at least my dad wasn't a television vacuum-cleaner salesman." Millie hung her head.

"And is that Sloane's father's job?" Miss Grimm asked.

"Yes, I think so. Wally said that he'd seen a man called Smedley Sykes selling vacuum cleaners on the home shopping channel."

"I see." Miss Grimm was beginning to get a clearer picture. "Well, it sounds to me, Millie, like you've realized your mistake. I think perhaps you could spend a couple of afternoons helping Wally with the mucking out down at the stables. And you can apologize to Sloane, if she ever bothers to arrive," Miss Grimm instructed.

"You mean I can keep my part in the play?" Millie looked up at Miss Grimm.

"Yes, of course." Ophelia nodded. "That was never in doubt."

"Oh, thank you, Miss Grimm!" Millie launched herself at the headmistress and gave her a hug.

"Steady on there, Millicent." Miss Grimm smiled. "I see you're taking your cues from your roommate these days."

Millie let go of Miss Grimm and sat back down on the couch.

By now, the clock on the wall indicated that it was ten past seven. There was a loud rumpus in Mrs. Derby's office and a knock on the study door. Miss Grimm went to open it.

"You're late, Sloane." The headmistress was stern.

Sloane made no apology. "I couldn't get my hair dryer to work."

"Sit there." Miss Grimm pointed at the couch next to Millie. "You're a very brave girl, Sloane Sykes."

"Thank you, Miss Grimm," Sloane replied. "I've been subjected to the most awful bullying."

"I didn't mean that." Ophelia took up her position

on the chair opposite. "You obviously don't believe in punctuality. Is that correct?"

Sloane had to think. *Punctuality*. Was that the same as punctuation? She couldn't remember.

"Yes, I do, Miss Grimm. I always use full stops and capital letters," Sloane replied at last.

Millie had to clamp her hand over her mouth for fear of bursting out laughing.

"Sloane, Millie has something she'd like to say to you." Miss Grimm chose at this stage to overlook Sloane's ignorance. But it had given her a plan that would be most satisfactory.

Sloane looked at Millie with an air of righteous indignation.

"I'm sorry that I insulted you, Sloane, by laughing about your mother and saying that your father had a silly job." Millie blinked.

"And?" Sloane glared.

"And what?" Millie was puzzled.

"And what are you going to do about it?" Sloane insisted. "Like, are you going to do my house chores for a week or carry my books or something?"

"She most certainly will not, Sloane Sykes." Miss Grimm's temper was beginning to fray. "Now, young lady, what do you have to say to Millie?"

Sloane shook her head. "Nothing. I didn't do anything. She started it and it was her fault she ended up with pudding on her head," she spat.

Ophelia's temperature was rising.

"I don't think so, Sloane. There are two sides to every story, and unless I hear an apology, heartfelt, from you in the next ten seconds, I will be handing your role in the school play to . . . Wally Whitstable, for all I care!" Miss Grimm roared.

Sloane's mouth gaped open.

"Ten, nine . . ." Miss Grimm began counting. She'd reached two when Sloane finally found her voice.

"Sorry, Millie," she seethed.

"Sorry for what?" Miss Grimm was secretly enjoying this a little.

"Sorry for tipping that goo on your head," Sloane added.

"Well, it was an apology, but I have to say I don't much believe you, Sloane." Miss Grimm shook her head. "This is not the first time your lack of manners has been brought to my attention. You can keep your part in the play for now, but if I hear one word, one single word, that says you have been less than kind or gracious or caring to anyone at this school, Wally will have that script in his hand before you have time to say 'mirror, mirror.' Do you understand me?" Miss Grimm stared at Sloane.

"Yes," Sloane replied.

"Yes, what?" Miss Grimm demanded.

"Yes, Miss Grimm."

"Better." Miss Grimm stood up. "Off you go now, Millie. Just report to Wally this afternoon and I'm sure he'll find you some jobs to do."

Sloane stood up to follow her.

"Where are you going, young lady?" Miss Grimm asked.

"Breakfast," Sloane replied. She wasn't a very fast learner.

"I don't think so," Miss Grimm said. "I'll have some porridge sent up for you. You have work to do."

"What work?" Sloane huffed.

"Well, for a start, I think we'll spend some time on the dictionary. At your age, you should definitely know the difference between *punctuality* and *punctuation*. I suspect copying out the entire *P* section of this will help." Miss Grimm pulled an enormous leather-bound Oxford dictionary from her bookcase. "You will report to my study every morning at seven and will remain here until lessons commence at half past eight, for as long as it takes."

"But that's child abuse!" Sloane wailed.

"Oh no, my dear girl." Miss Grimm shook her head.

"Think of it as extra tutoring, for free, and with the headmistress, no less. Now, why don't you sit yourself down over there." Ophelia pointed at the writing desk opposite her own. "I'll bring you some paper and a pen."

Chapter 34

Sloane appeared to be on her best behavior for the rest of the week. She attended her morning lessons with Miss Grimm and, despite looking like she'd sucked on a lemon, didn't complain at all—well, not to the other girls or teachers. She saved it all for her mother, who decided that her plan to bring Fayle unstuck was not only brilliant, it would also save her darling daughter from the clutches of the evil Miss Grimm.

During rehearsals, Sloane spent as much time with Lucas as she could.

"You're a brilliant Woodcutter," she complimented him.

"Thanks." Lucas didn't quite know what to make of his roommate's sister. Sep said that she was shallower than a kiddie wading pool, but she seemed okay.

"So, have you had a lot of tests lately?" she asked.

"We have a maths test every Tuesday. And there was a science exam yesterday," Lucas explained.

Sloane's brain was ticking. She needed to get her hands on a set of test papers.

"What's your maths teacher like?" She batted her eyes at Lucas.

"Really smart," Lucas replied, "but mad as a hatter. He's always forgetting things and bringing the wrong books, and I think last week he couldn't find our test papers."

"Oh really? He does sound a bit crazy." She smiled. "So on Tuesdays you have a test? That means you had it this morning."

"Yes." Lucas nodded. "I probably should be doing my homework between scenes. Sorry, it's just that we have quite a few assignments."

"I've got a much better idea." Sloane grinned like a fox in a henhouse. "Why don't you show me around a bit? Miss Reedy said that we won't be needed for at least another thirty minutes."

"I really should stay here and go over some

grammar." Lucas picked up a textbook from the bag at his feet.

"Oh, but I'd really love to have a look around, and Sep won't take me," Sloane pouted.

Lucas didn't want to leave the auditorium at all. But he'd also heard about Sloane's legendary tantrums, and the thought of her causing a scene was worse. "Okay, but it has to be quick," he agreed.

"Fine by me. Why don't you show me your classrooms?" Sloane purred.

Jacinta looked up from her position on the stage to see Sloane loop her arm through Lucas's and the pair head out of the theater. Her heart felt like a pounding lump of rock in her chest. The blinding lights didn't allow her to see that just as quickly as Sloane had grabbed him, Lucas had managed to pull his arm away, pretending he had an itchy nose.

Lucas showed Sloane around the classrooms in the main building. She seemed particularly keen to see where they had maths and science, which he thought a little strange, given that Septimus said she was not keen on academic studies at all.

Sloane lingered outside one of the rooms. "Can we go in?"

"I don't think we should." Lucas was keen to get back to the drama theater.

"Is there an alarm or something?" Sloane peered through the glass at the top of the door.

"No, it's just that the teachers don't really like us being in there when we don't have lessons," Lucas replied.

"All right," Sloane agreed. "Let's go back. This is boring."

Lucas was relieved. The pair walked along the corridor.

"Is there a ladies' loo around here anywhere?" Sloane asked.

"Um, I think it's back there, past the foyer." Lucas sighed. He didn't particularly want to wait for her.

"It's okay." Sloane smiled. "Why don't you go back and I'll join you shortly."

Lucas couldn't help himself and returned her smile. Maybe she wasn't really that painful after all.

"I'll see you in a bit," said Lucas.

Sloane turned and walked back toward the foyer. She waited until Lucas disappeared around the corner before rushing to the room where he'd said they had their maths lessons. The door was unlocked.

On the teacher's desk at the front of the room, atop a towering pile of papers, Sloane found exactly what she was after. The Weekly Quiz. Trouble was, she didn't have time to sit and change the papers now.

She'd have to do that later in the privacy of her own room—perhaps when Jacinta was at the gym training. She leafed through the stack and gathered up the tests from today. Fortunately, the professor was every bit as disorganized as she had hoped—his desk looked like an explosion in a paper factory. Sloane spent a couple of minutes rearranging papers from one side to the other—hopefully, by the time she had made the changes and returned the tests, the silly old man would be none the wiser. Sloane stuffed the papers into her backpack.

She smiled smugly. This was as easy as falling off a log.

Chapter 35

On Friday morning, Septimus Sykes and Lucas Nixon headed off to their maths lesson. Their teacher, Professor Pluss, welcomed the class with a smile that stretched from one side of his red face to the other. The boys couldn't remember ever seeing him look so happy.

"Greetings and salutations, lads." The professor moved to the front of the room. He walked over to his desk, where he put his hand on top of the pile of papers. "Today is a momentous day in the history of this fine school," he began.

"What's he talking about?" Lucas turned and whispered to Sep.

"Beats me," Sep replied.

"Today you have made me the proudest old prof on the planet. You see, boys, for the first time, certainly since I have been the mathematics master at this outstanding institution, which is over twenty years, every single member of this class has scored one hundred percent on the weekly quiz."

The boys smiled and laughed and congratulated themselves and one another.

"Quiet down, please. You must have all thought long and hard about your answers. By gosh, there was a good deal of crossing out, but even you, old Figgy"—Professor Pluss grinned at the oafish lad in the back row—"you must have been listening all that time I thought you were gazing longingly at the football field."

Lucas was puzzled. Figgy hadn't scored above fifty percent on the past four tests. And there were a couple of really tricky problems he was sure he'd messed up too.

Professor Pluss handed the papers back, then turned to the board and began to explain, in great detail and without time for any questions, how to find the circumference of a circle.

Sep put his paper to the side of his desk. Lucas leafed through his. It looked like his writing, but there was an answer he couldn't remember filling in. In fact, now that he was looking at it again, he was fairly certain he'd left that section blank.

"Excuse me, sir?" Lucas put up his hand and waited for the old man to turn around.

"What is it, Nixon?" The professor peered over the round spectacles perched on the end of his nose.

"Sir, I don't think this is all my work." Lucas held the test paper aloft.

Some of the other boys began to make similar noises.

"Nonsense, Nixon, you're not giving yourself enough credit there." The professor turned back to the board.

"But, sir, I'm pretty sure I left this answer blank," Lucas offered.

"Is there an answer there now?" The professor spoke with his back turned to the boys.

"Well, yes, sir," Lucas tried again.

"So you didn't leave it blank. Tell me, Nixon." The professor spun back around to face the group. "Tell me, what did you do at eleven minutes past two yesterday afternoon?"

Lucas thought for a moment and wondered if this was some kind of trick question. "I was in science class," he replied.

"Yes, but what *exactly* were you doing at eleven

minutes past two? Were you listening or speaking or marveling at the laws of gravity or the fact that we live on a spinning lump of rock in the middle of the universe?" the professor continued.

"I can't remember, sir." Lucas wasn't sure where this was heading.

"There you have it. Proof." The professor turned back to the board.

"I'm sorry, sir. Proof of what, exactly?" Lucas was feeling more and more confused by the second.

"My dear boy. Proof that you could well have written an answer on that page." He marched toward Lucas and picked up his paper. "And you probably forgot. We all forget things. In fact, we will forget far more than we ever remember. Did you know that statistically . . ." The professor was about to start one of his long lectures.

Lucas decided it was better to be quiet and leave things alone. But something wasn't right. The boys at Fayle didn't need to cheat. By and large, they were a smart enough bunch. They studied pretty hard too—it was just the way things were there. So why would anyone want to cheat just so the whole class scored one hundred percent?

"Why would anyone cheat for us?" Lucas asked Sep when they were on their way to English class.

"I don't know." Sep shook his head. "Make the old prof feel like a hero?"

"Yeah, maybe." The boys reached the entrance foyer. The classrooms in McGlintock Manor ran east and west, with science and maths on the west and English, history and geography on the eastern side. A magnificent staircase stood in the center of the building's entrance hall, rising one flight before splitting left and right. On the right-hand wall were portraits of Frederick Erasmus Fayle, the school's founder, and his successors. There were two more Fayles, and another man, before the picture of the current headmaster, Professor Winterbottom, whose portrait must have been painted early in his tenure, as his beaming face was wrinkle free. On the opposite wall in a large gilt frame, the Fayle School Charter was in full view for all to see.

"Oh, blast." Sep grimaced as they were about to climb the stairs.

"What's the matter?" Lucas asked.

"I forgot my assignment. It's in my locker. Will you wait? I won't be a minute." Sep handed Lucas his pile of books and sprinted back down the corridor.

Lucas set the tower of texts down on a high-backed chair that resembled a throne. He walked over to the charter and read from the top. He smiled at the school's motto—it was pretty funny, after all, to name a school Fayle. But it wasn't until he reached the bottom, clauses twenty-nine and thirty, that alarm bells began to ring. Lucas had an uncomfortable feeling that perhaps cheating had been happening for quite a while—but this time, the culprit had got rather carried away with themselves.

Sep returned and the two lads had to run to get to class before the bell. Lucas would have to wait to share his suspicions with his friend.

Chapter 36

September Sykes could not have been prouder when Sloane told her what she'd done.

"Oh yes," she gloated to her mother, "it won't be long now before the word gets out that more than twenty-five percent of boys have failed at Fayle. But it took loads of work, so you'd better thank me for it, Mummy," she hissed. "And I almost got caught taking the papers back." Sloane was whispering into the telephone. Although she thought she was alone in the common room, she never knew when someone might come in and overhear her conversation. "How's Granny?"

September attempted to sound sad. "Not doing too

well, I'm afraid. I went to see her yesterday afternoon and she looked rather peaky indeed. She seemed quite upset, poor old dear. But she did sign some very important documents for me. Have you heard of something called a power of attorney?"

She neglected to tell Sloane that the reason Henrietta had become so upset was that September had all but revealed her dastardly plan. She had told her about the suitcase, and that it was just so unfortunate that they'd found it but now it was gone again. Vanished out of sight. Poof—like magic. September thought the old bag might up and die right then and there, but her heart held out, and it was only when her stepdaughter-in-law promised another visit that Henrietta's face reddened and she looked set for another stroke.

"What shall we do with all that money?" September gloated, rubbing her manicured hands together.

"For a start, Mummy, I think we should go somewhere sunny—for good." Sloane smiled at the thought of her and her mother in their matching bikinis, lying in the sun with a butler attending to their every need.

Howie entered the common room. She frowned at Sloane, who seemed to have that phone perpetually stuck to her ear.

"Prep," Mrs. Howard ordered.

"But I've got play practice in ten minutes." Sloane smirked.

"Oh no you don't," Mrs. Howard replied. "Haven't you read the schedule, young lady? This afternoon, only Alice-Miranda, the prince and the woodcutter are needed. Oh, and Millie and Jacinta."

"Why does Millie get to go? She's *my* Magic Mirror," Sloane grouched.

"I don't know. But it says so on this here piece of paper." Howie waved the notice under Sloane's nose. She was still on the telephone.

Mrs. Howard took the handset from her. "Hello, Mrs. Sykes, it's Mrs. Howard. I'm afraid Sloane has to go to prep, so I'll tell her you said goodbye, will I?" And with that, Mrs. Howard hung up the phone.

"You've got no right . . . ," Sloane began, steam rising from her nostrils.

Mrs. Howard raised her eyebrows. Miss Grimm had asked her to keep a close eye on their newest student after the incident with Millie. She knew that any cheek, and Sloane would be out of the play. "Are you sure you want to say something?"

"I'm going." Sloane stalked off to her room.

Alice-Miranda, Jacinta and Millie were required on set for an extended rehearsal that afternoon. The group had walked to Fayle, but Miss Reedy had arranged for Charlie to pick them up in the school bus when they were finished, as it would be dark.

Miss Reedy was keen to get some of the lighting in place and, although the girls knew their parts well, she had decided it was easier to practice some scenes separately so the cast were completely confident. Lucas and Sep were also required to be there. The children had been rehearsing well, but as it was getting close to performance time, things needed to step up a little.

"Girls, I hope you don't mind, but we'll get started straightaway and then break for tea with the boys later. Then we'll do another hour or so and call it a night."

"That's lovely, Miss Reedy. It will give us a chance to catch up properly with Lucas and get to know Sep a bit better too." Alice-Miranda smiled.

Mr. Lipp greeted the group as they entered the auditorium. Today's suit made him look like a bloated canary.

"Hello, girls, Livinia." He had taken to using Miss Reedy's Christian name, which caused her to frown.

"Mr. Lipp." Miss Reedy nodded.

"Ready for some hard work?" Mr. Lipp asked.

"Oh yes, sir." Alice-Miranda beamed. "Where would you like to start?"

"I thought we'd go from your scene, Alice-Miranda, with the Prince," Miss Reedy directed.

And so the rehearsal began.

An hour later, the group trooped off to the dining room. The children sat together, while Mr. Lipp invited Miss Reedy to sit at the head table with Professor Winterbottom and his wife.

Sep grinned. "I think old Hairy's got a thing for your Miss Reedy."

"Really?" Millie screwed up her nose. "Well, that's gross. Anyway, she has a thing for our science teacher, Mr. Plumpton. You should see the two of them—he looks like a little beach ball and she's a string of spaghetti, but it's quite plain they adore one another."

"Perhaps they'll get married." Jacinta beamed. "I do love a wedding."

"Well, I imagine the next one you'll attend is my father's and Charlotte's," Lucas offered.

"Will I get invited?" Jacinta asked, wide-eyed.

"I should imagine so." Lucas grinned. And there it was again. Jacinta's heart fluttered in her chest.

"So, how are you all getting on with my sister?" Sep asked the group.

"Let's just say that she and I are hardly best friends," Millie replied.

"I think Sloane's a bit complicated," said Alice-Miranda. "I'm sure she has a heart of gold."

"You're kidding, Alice-Miranda," Jacinta snorted. "Sorry, Sep, but your sister isn't my favorite person either."

Septimus Sykes looked concerned. "Has she actually done anything wrong over there?"

"Well, she tipped her dessert on my head last week," Millie explained. "But I probably deserved it."

"And I caught her and your mother going through my things on the day she arrived," Jacinta added. "But they were probably just unpacking."

"I think you're both being far too kind." Sep shook his head. "You don't know her like I do."

"But she's your sister, Sep, you should stick up for her," Alice-Miranda said.

"I wish I could," Sep began. "She should be more grateful. The only reason either of us is at boarding school is because of our stepgrandmother Henrietta. She's paying for the lot. She's the sweetest lady, and my mother and father and sister treat her like garbage. I just wish I could see her."

"Where does she live?" Alice-Miranda asked.

"Well, that's the thing. She was meant to be able to

stay in the flat over Grandpa's old grocery shop, here in the village, for as long as she wanted. But Mum and Dad sold it and then she had a terrible stroke and now she lives in a retirement home called Golden Gates."

"But do you write to her?" Alice-Miranda asked.

"Yes, but she can't write back because of the stroke," Sep explained. "My sister is so hateful to her. But Grandpa adored her and so do I."

Alice-Miranda's brain was already in overdrive. She would call her parents as soon as she could and arrange for Sep to visit his granny. "Don't worry, Sep, I'm sure you'll get to see her very soon." She smiled.

Septimus Sykes had never met a girl like Alice-Miranda. She was so small, but seemed incredibly kind and smart too. He wished that *she* was his sister.

Millie changed the subject. "And how are you getting on with all the work, Lucas?"

"Good." Lucas grinned at Sep, who raised his eyebrows. "I scored one hundred percent on a maths test this week."

"Well done!" said Alice-Miranda.

"Problem was, so did everyone else," Lucas continued.

"What?" Mille wrinkled her nose. "The whole class got a hundred?"

"Was it an easy test?" Jacinta asked.

"No, that's just the point," Lucas answered. "There were some tricky questions."

"Was it multiple choice?" asked Millie.

Sep rejoined the conversation. "No. Lucas tried to tell Professor Pluss that the tests had been tampered with, but he would have none of it."

"Tampered with?" Alice-Miranda gasped. "Do you mean that someone changed the answers—they cheated?"

"Yes, someone cheated and we all got one hundred percent," Lucas confirmed.

"But why?" Millie asked.

"Well, Lucas and I have a bit of a theory." Sep frowned. "And it's probably been happening for years."

"Really?" Alice-Miranda's eyes were wide.

The children leaned in close. Lucas explained about the Fayle School Charter. He and Sep had come to the conclusion that the teachers must be cheating to make sure that the school stayed open. Maybe this time, Professor Pluss had just gotten carried away with himself and didn't realize that he'd changed all the papers.

"I asked Miss Reedy how Fayle came to be named and she told me all about the charter. That would be awfully sad, if what you say is true," Alice-Miranda said.

"I'd bet poor old Mr. Fayle would be turning in his grave," Millie added.

But Alice-Miranda found it hard to believe that a school like Fayle, with its wonderful teachers and high standards, would allow such a thing. It would mean that the teachers were plotting together, and she simply didn't believe this to be possible. Goodness, all the teachers she knew were honest and responsible. There had to be something else going on. They just needed to find out what it was.

Chapter 37

September Sykes put the telephone down and cupped her face in her hands. She couldn't believe what she had just heard. She dialed the number for the common room at Grimthorpe House.

"Hello, it's September Sykes. I must talk to my daughter, Sloane, immediately. It's an emergency," she informed Mrs. Howard.

"May I ask what type of emergency, Mrs. Sykes? I don't want to alarm your daughter," said Mrs. Howard.

"No, you may not ask, you nosey old parker," September growled.

Howie had a mind to hang the phone up immediately but thought better of it. September Sykes was the rudest, most vacuous mother she had ever come across in all her years in the boardinghouse. At times, that had been a hotly contested title, but this woman was the clear winner.

"Sloane." Mrs. Howard rapped on the door. "Your mother would like a word. She says that it's important."

Howie entered the dorm. Sloane was lying on her bed, admiring her nails.

"Can I take it in here?" Sloane noticed that Howie had the cordless telephone in her hand. Usually, it was strictly forbidden for the girls to take calls in their rooms, but this time, Howie relented and handed over the phone.

"Just don't be long," Howie instructed. "There are other girls who like to speak to their parents too."

Sloane turned her back to the house mistress and waited until she had left the room.

"Hello, Mummy," she said.

"Are you a complete idiot?" September began.

"What are you talking about?" Sloane snapped back.

"I've just got off the phone from your brother, and

apparently he's been doing so well, he got one hundred percent on his maths test this week," September informed her daughter.

"That's not possible," Sloane griped. "I changed all the papers."

"Yes, and whose paper did you copy from?" her mother asked.

"Septimus's, of course. Everyone knows he's as dumb as a rock," Sloane snarled.

"Well, I'm afraid that's not true. You see, everyone in the class scored one hundred percent!" September yelled. "And what were you thinking, changing all the answers to the same thing? I'm sure they wouldn't be very suspicious about that, now, would they?"

"How was I to know Sep's some kind of mathematical genius? I think he's an idiot!" Sloane roared back.

"Clearly you're wrong." September could hardly believe they were so close to their fortune and Sloane had made a complete mess of everything. "You have to do it again. And this time, don't use your brother's paper to copy from."

"Well, whose paper should I use, then?" Sloane demanded. "I don't know who's smart and who's not."

"As it happens, your brother commented that some

kid called Figgy almost never passes mathematics tests but got a hundred this time. So use his—but make sure that you mix them up a bit. For goodness' sake, do I have to do everything for this family?" September growled.

"Where's Daddy?" Sloane changed the subject. "I want to talk to him."

"Your idiot father is overseas checking on the development. But I have a feeling that it's not going according to plan either. Sloane—I don't have to tell you again what this will mean to our family. Now, can I rely on you this time?" Her mother's voice softened slightly.

"Of course, Mother." Sloane rolled her eyes. "But I can't do anything until next week."

"Why not?" September demanded.

"Because they only have their stupid test on Tuesday and it's the weekend. Duh!"

"There's no need to get smart with me, young lady. You'd better think about who you're talking to."

"And you'd better remember who's in the driver's seat here, Mother," Sloane snapped.

And with that, she terminated the call.

As it turned out, two more weeks passed before Sloane had her chance. Professor Pluss was so anxious about the boys not replicating their one hundred percent result that he didn't prepare a test for the coming week, and the week after that they had a sports carnival. But by the time they had their regular weekly quiz again, Pluss was confident the lads would not let him down.

Chapter 38

Professor Pluss stood outside the headmaster's study trembling. He couldn't believe that in a career spanning more than thirty years, this was what he would be remembered for.

The campus was abuzz. Pluss had asked two of his colleagues to re-mark the papers. They had both come back to him, faces solemn, heads bowed.

Someone must have leaked the news to Professor Winterbottom, who had summoned Pluss for an urgent meeting first thing this morning. Even old Hedges, the gardener, had sneered as Herman Pluss took his walk of shame to the headmaster's study.

Miss Quigley, the headmaster's personal assistant,

shuddered as he entered the room. She was poring over a large document and had just retrieved a gigantic magnifying glass from the bottom desk drawer.

A woman renowned for her confidential manner, she had been with Professor Winterbottom as long as he'd been in charge. "How could you?" she murmured under her breath.

Herman thought his knees would buckle any moment.

"He'll see you now."

For a moment, Herman wondered how she knew that the headmaster was ready for him, but he suspected that after almost forty years together, they likely shared some sort of telepathic messaging system.

The door opened and Professor Winterbottom asked Professor Pluss inside.

"Take a seat. There." The headmaster pointed. Professor Winterbottom's dog, Parsley, who spent his days curled up in a basket in the headmaster's study, growled as Professor Pluss sat down.

"I hear you have something to tell me?"

But Professor Winterbottom didn't have to ask. He already knew. The whole school knew. Something as monumental as this would never remain a secret. It had never happened before, and it would certainly never happen again.

"I . . . don't know what to tell you, sir. . . . My class . . . eighty percent of them . . ." Herman gulped.

"Yes, eighty percent of them have what?" Professor Winterbottom had so far managed to keep calm.

"Eighty percent of them have . . ." Herman clutched his face in his hands, hardly daring to say the word. "They've failed. There it is. I've said it."

"How can a class go from one hundred percent success two weeks ago to . . . this?" Professor Winterbottom held one of the offending papers aloft. "Yes, I know all about it. Your colleagues would hardly keep something like this a secret. In fact, they all know— the boys, the teachers. Do *you* know what this means, Pluss?"

Herman Pluss looked up and nodded.

"You, you and your vanity, have brought this great school to its knees. Do you know what it says in that charter out there?" Wallace pointed at the wall where the Fayle School Charter hung in all its ancient glory. "It says that if more than twenty-five percent of students fail *any* test, the school must be closed within twenty-eight days."

"But, sir." Herman shuddered. "Surely, that can't really be true. Can it?"

"It most certainly is. I warned you, Pluss, about all those weekly quizzes. I told you they weren't necessary and that one day you might come unstuck. But you assured me. Your teaching methods were inscrutable. You were the best teacher this place had ever seen. Well, look what you've done." Professor Winterbottom's head looked like a pressure cooker about to explode.

There was a knock on the door. It opened and Miss Quigley entered.

"Sir, may I interrupt?" she asked. "I've found something."

"Well, unless it will save the school . . ." Professor Winterbottom sighed so deeply it felt like a draft in the room.

"Well, sir, I think you will be very happy to see this." Miss Quigley unfolded the original copy of the Fayle School Charter onto her boss's football-field-sized desk. She produced the magnifying glass from her skirt pocket and pointed her manicured finger at the very bottom of the page.

"There, sir." Wallace Winterbottom and Herman Pluss leaned in closely to look.

"I can't see a thing. It looks like a squiggly line," the headmaster complained.

"That's what I thought too. But, sir, if you look

{246}

closely—" She held the magnifying glass over the end of the line and read aloud. "'Clause thirty of the Fayle School Charter can be revoked at any time, at the discretion of the heir to the Fayle estate. In the event that there is no living heir, the school must close and be sold, with the proceeds going to the Queen's Trust for Children.'"

"Heavens, that's it!" Professor Winterbottom grabbed Miss Quigley in a bearlike embrace. "Woman, you're a genius!" He then quickly let her go, embarrassed by his uncharacteristic outburst of affection. "But how did we miss this?"

"Well, sir, it's not on the charter in the foyer. I suspect that the edge of the page was cut off to fit it in the frame," Miss Quigley remarked. "From the looks of this dusty old thing, it hasn't been out of the safe in many years."

"But who is the heir?" Wallace Winterbottom paced the floor. Not that it was an easy thing to do in his office, which was crammed full of furniture, books and other paraphernalia, including a rather large cabinet containing a bizarre collection of taxidermic birds. He began to think out loud. "Fayle was founded by Frederick Fayle, and the next headmaster was his only son, George, and then I think the next head was George's son Erasmus."

"Sir, if I may say something?" Professor Pluss asked.

The headmaster was terse. "What?"

"Didn't Erasmus, his wife and his daughter perish in some terrible accident? I seem to recall when I was a boy and lived in Downsfordvale, there was a story about the headmaster of Fayle and his family passing in tragic circumstances. I can't remember much else."

"Yes, I've read about that somewhere too. There was another man who came in then. The headmaster after Erasmus was Rigby Lloyd. You'd remember him. He employed me. And that's how I became headmaster so early on. Rigby was working in here one night when the poor fellow dropped dead of a heart attack."

"So are there any Fayles left, sir?" Miss Quigley asked.

"I think there was another daughter who survived. But she'd be very old—if she's still alive, that is." Professor Pluss tapped his right forefinger to his lip.

"We'd better hope she's alive and well, and find her quick smart," Professor Winterbottom announced.

"Helloooo?" a voice drifted in from the office outside. "Is anyone home?"

Miss Quigley opened the study door.

"Oh, there you are. I need to see the headmaster."

September Sykes stood towering in the doorway on her six-inch red heels.

"Can I help you?" The professor had not yet had the pleasure of meeting Mrs. Sykes, as it was Sep's father who had taken the boy for his entrance test and interview. September had been busy that morning at the nail salon.

"I'm September," she cooed.

Professor Winterbottom had no idea what that meant at all, and responded with a blank look and a shake of his head.

"September Sykes. Septimus's mother." She smiled.

"Oh, of course, Mrs. Sykes," said Professor Winterbottom apologetically. "I'm afraid we're a little bit busy at the moment, Mrs. Sykes. Is it an urgent matter you've come about?"

"You might think so." September nodded. "You see, I've really come to find out how much this is all worth." She waved her arms around.

The headmaster looked confused. "Worth? Do you mean the school fees?"

"No, no, no, silly headmaster." September was enjoying this. "I mean the school. Fayle. The whole place."

"I have no idea what you're talking about." Professor Winterbottom was growing very uncomfortable.

"It's just that, well, I know what happens when more than twenty-five percent of boys at this school fail a test. And I've heard that's just happened. So I want to know what it's worth?"

"I can't for a moment imagine that's any of your business, Mrs. Sykes." The headmaster was appalled.

September Sykes entered the study. She walked over to the antique globe that stood under the window and gave it a spin. "Oh, isn't that fun?" she giggled.

Professors Winterbottom and Pluss and Miss Quigley could not take their eyes off this woman with her long blond curls and garish red dress which hugged every curve.

"Mrs. Sykes, I think it might be best if you left," the headmaster suggested.

"Now, why would I do that?" September walked toward the group, reached forward and grabbed Professor Winterbottom's tie, pulling him closer. Her sickly perfume clouded his head and he soon felt quite faint. She let go and walked around the desk, where she sat in his green leather chair. "What do you think?" She placed the professor's reading glasses on the end of her nose. "Does the school look suit me? No, no. Not my thing at all, teaching. Really just for dull old bores, education."

"Mrs. Sykes." Professor Winterbottom regained use of his vocal cords. "You need to leave immediately."

"No." September shook her head. "You need to sit down and have a look at this." She rummaged around in her oversized pewter-colored handbag and produced what appeared to be a legal document. "You see, I heard you before, when I was out in the other room there. You can stop looking for the heir to the Fayle family. Because you've found her. And this"— she waved the power of attorney under the professor's nose—"is all the proof you need. Granny Henrietta Sykes—she's the one you were talking about—well, she married my darling husband's father just a few years back. She was a Fayle, you know. But she's not well, and she's very old, and she insisted I look after things for her. So there you are."

"Oh, thank heavens, Mrs. Sykes. We were worried that we'd never find the heir in time and then the school would have no choice other than to close at the end of the term. But now . . ."

"But now *what?*" September sneered. "You'll be closing, all right. I've arranged for the estate agent to meet me here this morning. I can't imagine how many millions this place is worth, but I'm going to have lots of fun spending them."

Professor Pluss burst into tears. Miss Quigley had to suppress the urge to strangle September on the spot. The headmaster gulped.

"Professor Pluss—you need to go to class. Miss Quigley—some tea." He indicated the door. "Mrs. Sykes and I have a lot to talk about."

"No, we don't, unless you want to tell me how wonderful Septimus is. But if you think I'll change my mind, you're wrong, old man." September folded her arms in front of her.

Chapter 39

Word had spread quickly about the trouble at Fayle. Professor Winterbottom had spent an hour with September Sykes trying to change her view about enforcing the school's closure, but he was no match for her when she had millions on her mind. He suggested that they ask Mr. Sykes in to talk about things, but she said he was overseas working and couldn't be contacted. September was determined to show her husband a thing or two about making money.

At Winchesterfield-Downsfordvale, Millie and Alice-Miranda were talking about the recent turn of events.

"None of this makes any sense at all." Millie was lying facedown on her bed with her arms tucked under her chin.

"It's strange, isn't it, that on one test the boys all score full marks, and then only a couple of weeks later they fail. I have a very bad feeling about all this," Alice-Miranda decided. "Sep and Lucas must have been wrong about the cheating."

"And imagine the Sykeses being the heirs." Millie rolled her eyes. "I mean, Sep's lovely, but Sloane, urgh."

"Sep really loves it at school too. Maybe he can talk his mother into keeping it open," Alice-Miranda suggested.

At that moment, Sloane Sykes appeared in the open doorway. "I don't think so. Mummy and I don't care about that stupid school. Sep will just have to find somewhere else to go."

"Oh, hello, Sloane." Alice-Miranda smiled. "Would you like to come in?"

"Why?" Sloane retorted.

"I thought you might like to work on your lines with us," said Alice-Miranda.

"It's all right, Sloane, I'm sure you're way too busy working out how you'll squander all those millions."

The last thing Millie wanted was to spend any more time with Sloane than she had to.

"I suppose our play next week will be Fayle's last hurrah," Sloane laughed.

"Well, perhaps not." Alice-Miranda smiled. "Maybe your mother will think about the school and how important it is, and all that history. I mean, it's a big thing to close down a place that has educated so many boys. It's strange too, how one week the boys all scored one hundred percent on their test and then the very next test they failed."

"Yes, I wonder how that could have happened?" Sloane couldn't help herself. Her voice was dripping with sarcasm. "Amazing, isn't it?"

Millie sat up. She watched Sloane. There was something about the twitch around her mouth— Millie had taken to reading about body language and knew this could be a sign of lying. When Sloane scratched her neck (another dead giveaway), Millie couldn't keep quiet any longer.

"You did it, didn't you?" Millie leapt from her bed to confront the girl.

"What?" Sloane retorted. "I didn't do anything." Sloane's eyes darted around the room.

"I remember, when we were at Fayle a couple of

{255}

weeks ago, you went missing for ages and we were supposed to practice our scene. When you came back, you told Miss Reedy that you'd got lost. I bet you were changing the answers on the papers." Millie's face was bloodred.

"You've got a very good imagination, little one," Sloane snapped. "And so what? Even if I did, you'll never prove it."

"I'll tell Miss Grimm," Millie threatened.

"Go ahead," Sloane challenged her. "You can't prove it, and then you're just going to look like a little snitch." Sloane turned and stalked off.

Millie fizzed with rage. "She's foul. We have to find a way to prove that she cheated."

Alice-Miranda walked over and stood calmly beside her friend. She looked at the clock beside her bed. It was just after two p.m. on Sunday afternoon. "I think we should go and see Miss Hephzibah. A ride in the countryside will do us both a world of good."

"I agree. I don't want to hang around here with *that* next door." Millie began to change into her riding gear.

Not half an hour later, the girls were sitting in the kitchen at Caledonia Manor having tea and scones.

"There's a terrible disaster at Fayle," Alice-Miranda informed their friend.

"Really?" Hephzibah raised her veil slightly so she could sip her tea. She still hadn't taken it off in front of Millie, although the child seemed much more comfortable in her presence now.

"The boys in Professor Pluss's maths class failed a test and now the school is going to be closed," Alice-Miranda continued.

"Yes, it's to do with some silly old rule in the Fayle School Charter that if any more than twenty-five percent of boys fail any test, then the school must close and be returned immediately to the eldest heir of Frederick Fayle," Millie added. "And you wouldn't believe who that is. . . ."

Hephzibah nodded thoughtfully.

"It's a family called the Sykeses. Sloane Sykes started at our school just this term, and she's awful," said Millie. "And it's more than likely that she took the papers and changed the answers, and the school's going to close because of her cheating. It's all so obvious, but there's just no way to prove it."

Alice-Miranda chimed in. "Her brother, Sep, is such a lovely boy. He's devastated about the school closing. But Mrs. Sykes won't reconsider. She wants it all sold straightaway." Alice-Miranda shook her head. "I telephoned Mummy and Daddy and asked if there was anything that could be done. Daddy even sent over to Fayle for a copy of the charter, and he said that there was a secret clause in the smallest of print saying that if the heir said the school could stay open then it would, and they could make sure the silly clause was revoked for good, but Mrs. Sykes is determined that she and her husband get the money. They're only in line anyway because Mr. Sykes's father married one of the Fayles. A lady called Henrietta—"

Hephzibah clutched her chest.

Alice-Miranda rose in alarm. "Are you all right?"

"What were you going to say?" Hephzibah whispered. "About the Fayle woman?"

"Well, she's in a nursing home now and the Sykeses have her power of attorney, which means that they get to make all the decisions for her about money and things like that."

Hephzibah breathed freely at last. "It sounds like someone needs to do something." She stood and walked to the playroom and returned with a shoe box. She began to unpack its contents onto the table.

"I think it's time I told you girls a story," Hephzibah said.

"Oh yes, I love stories." Alice-Miranda clapped her hands together. Millie looked up from buttering her scone.

Hephzibah took a sip of tea, as if steeling herself for the task ahead. Then she began. "Once upon a time, long, long ago, there was a little girl called Hephzibah Caledonia . . ."

Chapter 40

Alice-Miranda and Millie returned from Hephzibah's in a flurry of excitement. Alice-Miranda telephoned her parents immediately.

"Hello, Mummy." The tiny child was buzzing like a bee in a jar.

Cecelia Highton-Smith smiled. "Oh, hello, darling, how are you getting on?"

"I'm very well, thank you, Mummy. How is everyone at home?"

"Wonderful, darling, although Granny Bert is getting rather forgetful. I popped in to see her the other morning and she kept calling me Charlotte. It's sad to see her getting old," Cecelia mused. "And Mrs.

Oliver's been making some excellent progress with her organic vegetables. Shilly's got the place shining like a gold watch and I saw Lily and the children yesterday. They can't wait for you to come home for the holidays. But everyone's going to the play at the end of the week."

Alice-Miranda loved to hear all the news but that day she felt about ready to burst with her own. "Mummy," she interrupted, "I need to talk to you about something very important."

Cecelia was taken aback by her little daughter's tone. "Are you all right, darling? Is everything okay there at school? Miss Grimm hasn't had a relapse, has she?"

"Oh, Mummy, of course not. You are a funny one. Miss Grimm is very happy. Well, except about what's happening at Fayle. But that's why I'm calling. Millie and I need your help. You see . . ." Alice-Miranda spent the next ten minutes telling her mother a story that seemed more like something from a fairy tale.

After some reassurances and promises from her mother, Alice-Miranda hung up the telephone. Perhaps there might be a way to save Fayle after all.

Chapter 41

Millie and Alice-Miranda decided to give Sloane another chance to confess. At the final dress rehearsal, they told Jacinta, Sep and Lucas what they suspected. Lucas said that it all made sense. Sloane had made him take her for a walk around the school a few weeks ago, and she had particularly wanted to know about the classrooms and the teachers and where they kept their marking. He'd told her everything he knew and left her alone after she made the excuse that she needed to go to the toilet and insisted he go back to the rehearsal.

"If she admits it, then we can go to Professor

Winterbottom and stop the school being closed," said Sep.

"Have you talked to your father about any of this?" Alice-Miranda asked.

"No, he's away overseas working. I've tried to get in touch with him, but the phone just rings out," Sep replied. "Dad might try and put a stop to it all. But I don't really know. Like I said, sometimes I think I was born on another planet and the aliens decided to leave me with the Sykeses as a bit of a sick joke."

Alice-Miranda smiled. She couldn't imagine what it would be like to feel as if you didn't belong in your own family.

"I say we confront her today," Millie decided.

They all agreed.

Right then, a scene with the dwarfs returning home from work was being rehearsed and Alice-Miranda, Millie, Sep and Lucas weren't required. Jacinta had to stay back; being the narrator meant she didn't really get a break the whole time. The others watched as Sloane walked away from where she had been sitting and wandered upstairs to the foyer. Seeing a perfect chance, the children followed her. As she emerged from the ladies' toilet, they surrounded her.

"What do you lot want?" Sloane stared through narrowed eyes.

"Sloane, you need to do the right thing about the tests," Sep told her.

Sloane rolled her eyes and folded her arms in front of her. "I don't know what you're talking about."

"Yes, you do. You stole the tests and changed the answers. I bet that the first time, you decided to use my paper to copy from because you're always telling me how stupid I am. It must have upset you when everyone scored one hundred percent."

"You haven't got any proof. I didn't change your stupid tests. Anyway, it's too late to stop things now. Mummy said that she's already got a buyer for the place," Sloane spat.

"You'll get what's coming to you," Millie threatened.

Sloane laughed. "And what's that, millions of dollars, you little twit?" She pushed her way through the children and strutted back to the hall. Sep and Lucas followed her.

Millie was grim. "She's had her chance."

Alice-Miranda agreed.

Chapter 42

September Sykes had refused to listen to the pleas of Professor Winterbottom, her own son and even the gardener, who had all begged her to think again. But with Smedley safely out of the way working on the property business, there was nothing that would stand in her way. September didn't see any need for her husband to know a thing until the deal was done. Soon the Sykeses would be rich. They would be invited to the best parties, they would have the most important friends, and September could buy anything she ever wanted. No doubt there'd be an invitation to Lawrence Ridley's celebrity wedding too.

Meanwhile, the children had been rehearsing for weeks. But as the play drew closer, it seemed that a cloud of gloom had descended over the village of Winchesterfield. The cast all knew their lines by heart, the costumes were dazzling and the backdrops superb, but there was one thing missing—excitement. The usual theatrical buzz had all but disappeared.

The days leading up to the performance were almost unbearable as the students and staff contemplated the closure of Fayle forever. Only Alice-Miranda and Millie seemed anything like their usual selves.

"Come on, everyone," Alice-Miranda pleaded when the cast gathered together before the curtain went up on opening night. "Cheer up! It's not the end of the world."

"No, but it's the end of our school." Grumpy the dwarf frowned.

"Well, maybe there's a bit of magic left in the old place yet." Alice-Miranda smiled.

"Can I come to Winchesterfield-Downsfordvale next term?" the little boy playing the role of Happy asked.

"Hey, that's not as silly as it sounds!" Millie smiled and winked at Alice-Miranda. "We can ask Miss

Grimm. I'd love to know what she thinks about that idea."

"I already have asked her," Miss Reedy informed the group. "Never say never."

"Only so long as we don't have to wear dresses," Lucas added.

There was a collective giggle and the mood began to lift.

"Well, come on, everyone, I can see all the parents arriving." Alice-Miranda poked her nose through the side curtain. "Look, there's Mummy and Aunt Charlotte and Mrs. Oliver and Shilly and Daisy . . . Oh goodness, I think everyone's come to watch." She squeezed Millie's arm.

"There's my mother and father too." Millie winked at them through the gap in the curtains.

Jacinta looked over the top of the girls' heads. She'd heard earlier in the day that her mother had telephoned Mrs. Derby to say she was stuck in Monaco. Her father had said that he would try to get there, but as yet there was no sign. It didn't matter anyway. She hadn't reserved them any tickets.

Jacinta turned to Alice-Miranda. "Where's your father and Mr. Ridley?"

"They'll be along soon. They're just getting something sorted," Alice-Miranda replied.

Mr. Lipp bustled onto the stage and began ushering the girls and boys away from the curtains. "Come along now, children. We're starting in five minutes."

Miss Reedy and Mr. Lipp had the children form a circle backstage.

"Well, girls and boys, this is it. You've been rehearsing for weeks now, and I know you're all going to do a wonderful job this evening. You are a credit to yourselves and your schools." Miss Reedy wiped a tear that had formed in the corner of her eye.

"I couldn't agree more, Livinia," Mr. Lipp began. "It's been a pleasure working with you all. I will miss . . ." Mr. Lipp began to blubber like a baby.

Miss Reedy pulled a tissue from her pocket and handed it to him. He blew his nose like an off-key trumpet.

"And we've had the best time working with you too," said Alice-Miranda, smiling at the teachers. She glanced around the circle at the other students. "Now, I think we owe it to Miss Reedy and Mr. Lipp to put on the best performance of our lives. Three cheers for the teachers—hip hip hooray, hip hip hooray, hip hip hooray! And one cheer for us—HOORAY!"

Chapter 43

"B"reak a leg," Millie whispered to Sloane as she took up her position behind the Magic Mirror. "I hope *you* break *your* leg," Sloane spat back.

Millie sat in the chair behind her mirror. Charlie had helped to build the props, and he'd done an especially wonderful job with this. He'd used a reflective surface that allowed Millie's face to fade in and out whenever she spoke to the Queen. Mr. Plumpton had also been involved, giving Mr. Charles some newfangled materials that he'd been working with.

Miss Grimm and Mr. Grump took their seats beside Professor Winterbottom and his wife, Deidre, in the middle of the third row. The theater was almost full, except for one empty seat in the center of the second row. The lights began to dim.

"Hang on a tick. I'm not in my seat yet!" September Sykes teetered at the top of the stairs. The entire audience swiveled their heads in unison to see the outline of a woman in a minuscule dress, with more hair than your average lion, trying to navigate her way to the front. "Put the lights on, please," September asked in a syrupy voice.

There was a gasp as the parents and teachers squinting through the darkness realized exactly who the woman in the too-tight dress was.

"That's her. The one who's making the school close. . . . She's vile. . . . It's disgraceful . . ."

When nothing happened, September asked again. "Put the lights on, NOW!" This time, there was not even a touch of sweetness in the request.

The poor young teacher at the lighting desk almost jumped out of his skin. He brought up the house lights. The audience couldn't take their eyes off September. She bounced and flounced to the second row and edged past the seated guests all the way to the middle, trampling more than one set of toes as she went.

September took their gasps and groans as compliments.

"Thank you, thank you." She finally reached her seat. "You can turn the lights off now," she shouted.

A drumroll rumbled and the curtains went up.

"Once upon a time, long, long ago, a beautiful queen wished more than anything to be blessed with a child," Jacinta narrated.

"You might want to wish for something less bothersome," September quipped.

Ashima, in the role of Snow White's mother, stood at an open window with her needlework. She ignored the heckle and continued with her lines. The scene finished and the curtains closed, amid hearty clapping from the audience.

"She wasn't that good," September said under her breath.

As the curtains opened again, the Evil Queen stood in the center of the stage, her back to the audience. Her Magic Mirror sat on an elaborate dressing table facing the audience.

"Sloane!" September called, and waved. "That's my girl up there. Mummy's here, darling, front and center."

The audience were fast losing their patience with this horrid woman.

Sloane was perfect in the part. She primped and preened. She checked her nails and brushed her hair and spent rather more time than Miss Reedy remembered from the rehearsals before she spoke to the mirror.

"Mirror, mirror, on the wall, who is the fairest of them all?" Sloane gazed lovingly at her own reflection.

Suddenly the mirror swirled and Millie's face appeared.

"Thou, Queen. There is none fairer than you," the mirror replied, and with that, Millie disappeared.

"Bravo, bravo!" September shouted.

"Keep it down, woman." It was Hedges, Fayle's gardener, who had the dubious pleasure of sitting beside her.

The play continued. The audience clapped and cheered for Snow White at the end of her scene with the Woodcutter and laughed and laughed when she was found by the dwarfs. In no time at all, it was intermission.

September turned to the man sitting on her left. "Isn't she adorable?"

"Yes, she's a special one, that Snow White," he replied. It was Charlie and, next to him was Wally from Winchesterfield-Downsfordvale.

"Not that brat," September grizzled. "I meant the Queen—my daughter. She's lovely."

"That's one word for her," Wally quipped. *But per-*

haps not the first one that springs to mind, he thought.

Intermission lasted just a couple of minutes. Alice-Miranda grabbed what looked to be a script from backstage and handed it to Jacinta. "Use this one from now on. There's no time to explain. Just go with it at the end—and don't be frightened. It's very important."

Jacinta had no idea what her friend was talking about. And she didn't have time to look either. In a blink, the sets were changed and the curtain went up again.

"I haven't even had time for a bathroom break," September complained. "No champagne either. What sort of a play is this?"

"A school play, love," Hedges leaned over and whispered, rolling his eyes at the dim-witted woman.

The scenes with Snow White and the dwarfs were wonderful. Poor old Sneezy's allergies were playing up more than ever, and at one point he sneezed fifteen times in a row before they could continue.

"And here he goes again, and again, oh, now for something different . . ." Grumpy's improvisations delighted the audience, who were in hysterics.

There were boos for the Evil Queen as she tricked Snow White into eating her poison apple and sniffles when Snow White was found by her little friends and lifted into her glass coffin. Charlie, Wally and Hedges all produced large handkerchiefs to catch their torrents of tears. And then the Handsome Prince arrived to save the beautiful princess. When she awoke, the auditorium filled with cheers. The Prince's proposal had all the ladies swooning. Sep made a very handsome suitor indeed.

At last, it was nearing the final scene. The Evil Queen appeared onstage, fawning about all over herself.

"Mirror, mirror, on the wall, who's the fairest of them all?" she demanded.

Sloane turned her back to the mirror and gazed out at the audience. There was a loud gasp. This time, it wasn't Millie in the mirror.

"Look!" Wally called out. "It's the witch. It's the witch from the woods. Ahhhhh!" The young lad clung to Charlie beside him. The whole audience drew in a collective gasp.

There in the mirror was Hephzibah, her scarred face hidden by her black veil.

"Jacinta," Alice-Miranda whispered offstage. "Just say it."

"Dear Queen," Jacinta looked at the script. She was completely bewildered. "Your cheating ways and evil lies have earned you now the greatest prize. A dear, dear friend has come to speak about the havoc you did wreak."

"That's not how it goes." Sloane looked over to where Jacinta was standing. Miss Reedy was on the other side of the wings, flapping her arms about wildly. "Who are you, anyway?" Sloane demanded as she turned back to the mirror.

"She's the witch from the woods," Wally shouted. "Everyone knows that!"

"What witch?" Sloane folded her arms in front of her.

And then the mirror spoke.

"I know what you have done, Sloane Sykes."

Sloane gasped. "I haven't done anything." She turned back to face her accuser. "I don't know what you're talking about."

"I'm afraid you do, Sloane Sykes," Hephzibah continued. "You changed those papers. You made the boys fail."

The audience had no idea what was going to happen next. Sloane began to shake. She did not know who this woman was, but she certainly didn't like her tone.

"It wasn't me. I didn't do anything," Sloane protested.

"I don't believe you, Sloane Sykes. And do you know what happens to little girls who tell lies? Would you like to find out?" Hephzibah was shaking too.

Sloane started to cry. She spun around and pointed straight at her mother. "It was her. It was all her idea. She made me take the papers and change the answers. She said that we would be rich. Like all of *you!*"

September Sykes sat with her mouth open like a stunned goldfish. The young teacher on the spotlight wheeled it around and suddenly there was September: a deer in the headlights, in a tiny green dress with nowhere to go.

"I don't know what she's talking about," September blurted. "She's such a liar. Aren't you, Sloane? Always telling lies. Why do you think I sent her to boarding school in the first place?"

The audience drew in another collective gasp.

"I hate you, Mummy!" Sloane screeched, and fled from the stage.

Alice-Miranda coughed and nodded at Jacinta, who could hardly believe what she had just seen. Hephzibah was gone and the mirror was just a mirror.

Jacinta cleared her throat. "The Evil Queen was banished from the kingdom and Snow White and her Prince were married and lived happily . . . ever . . . after. . . ."

There was a pause as the children gathered their wits about them and flooded back onto the stage for the wedding party. The music struck up and Snow White and her Prince danced left and right, to much cheering and stamping of feet.

The scene ended, the cast took their bows and the audience clapped loudly. As the noise died down, Alice-Miranda invited Miss Reedy and Mr. Lipp to join the group, where they were both presented with enormous bunches of flowers. The cast bowed once more and then stood in two lines, facing an expectant audience.

Professor Winterbottom moved from his seat to the microphone.

"Ladies and gentlemen, girls and boys, I'm sure you will agree with me that we have seen an astonishing performance here this evening—not exactly as expected, but fantastic just the same."

September Sykes was wondering how on earth she could get out of the building. She needed to find her sniveling daughter and they needed to leave, as quickly as possible.

"I'm sure you've all heard about the recent real-life dramas here at Fayle. For a while, we thought the school would be closing at the end of the term, but as you saw tonight, that's not going to happen. And I'd personally like to thank Mrs. Sykes for that. You see, if she hadn't tested the waters, so to speak, we might never have read the very fine, fine print, which actually told us that clause thirty of the Fayle School Charter could at any time be revoked by the oldest living relative of Frederick Fayle. Therefore, I do hope tonight that we can repeal that somewhat silly old rule, and while I can assure you that the boys at Fayle will not fail, we will no longer have that hanging over our heads."

"But I have Granny Henrietta's power of attorney," September spat. "I made her sign it . . . I mean, she insisted I have it." September stood up. "And I'm not changing that rule. There will come a day when these boys *will* fail, and then all this"—she waved her arms like a model from *The Price Is Right*—"will belong to me."

"It may be true that you have acquired your step-mother-in-law's power of attorney, Mrs. Sykes, but you should check your facts. It seems that Henrietta is not Fred Fayle's oldest living relative," said Professor Winterbottom.

September gasped. "What are you talking about, you silly old man?"

"If you'd take your seat, Mrs. Sykes, I'd like to invite Alice-Miranda Highton-Smith-Kennington-Jones to speak to us. I think she might be able to shed some light on this mystery."

Alice-Miranda stepped forward to the microphone. Professor Winterbottom adjusted it downward.

"Thank you, Professor. Hello, everyone. It's so lovely to be here tonight. If you would allow me, I'd like to tell you a story. You see, on the first night back this term, the girls in my house at school told me a tale about a witch who lived in the woods. That weekend, I went out riding with Millie and Susannah and Sloane and, well, I have a very naughty pony who loves vegetables. . . ."

"You can say that again," Mr. Greening, the Highton-Smith-Kennington-Joneses' gardener, called from the audience. He received a sharp jab in the ribs from Mrs. Greening beside him.

"Well, we had a lovely ride and a delicious picnic, and then, when we were all on our way home, Bonaparte sniffed out a vegetable patch, so the girls went one way and I went another, and I ended up meeting a wonderful lady and I'd like to introduce her to you all now." Alice-Miranda looked to the wings and beckoned with her right hand. Millie helped Hephzibah walk slowly onto the stage. No longer dressed in

{279}

black, Hephzibah wore a lovely dress of purple and red, with a dainty hat and small net veil covering her face.

"Everyone, this is my dear friend, Miss Hephzibah Caledonia Fayle. She'd like to say something to you all."

The audience gasped.

"She's not a Fayle!" September blurted. "I've got the family tree and she's not on it." But a sick feeling rose in September's stomach as she remembered that there was a corner of the document missing.

Hephzibah stood beside Alice-Miranda, who turned and gave her a gentle hug. Professor Winterbottom reached forward and raised the microphone.

"Hello, everyone." Hephzibah's voice wavered. "As you've just heard, my name is Hephzibah Caledonia Fayle." She spoke slowly and deliberately. "I am an old woman who has spent most of her life being frightened. I have hidden from the world, too scared to show my face. In fact, everyone believed that I had perished in the fire which claimed my beloved parents many years ago, and I was happy for them to think that. And so, I became a sort of legend—the witch in the woods with her hundreds of cats. But this little girl, this wonderful little girl"—Hephzibah leaned down and kissed the top of Alice-Miranda's head—"has shown me how to live again. She has made me laugh and cry, and she's fed me some delicious chocolate brownies and introduced me to her delightful friend Millie.

"You see, my younger sister Henrietta gave up the best years of her life to be with me. Together, we made a life—and never left our home. Percy Sykes, a kind and wise man, delivered our groceries for years. He thought Henrietta lived at the manor alone, as I always hid from view if anyone ever came in. I hid in the playroom, of all places. It was where I felt safest. When Percy lost his own dear wife, over time he and my sister fell in love.

"After all that Henrietta had sacrificed, she deserved to be happy, but I told her that if she married Percy, I didn't want to see her again. My scars had made me selfish and hard. But that's not how the story will end. Today, with the help of Alice-Miranda's father and uncle, I have visited my sister. She is recovering from a stroke. We sat and we held hands and we cried tears of joy. I would also like to say, that while my great-great-grandfather Frederick Fayle was obviously a clever and visionary man, he wrote a very silly charter, and therefore, I hereby repeal clause thirty from this day forth.

"So I am sorry to disappoint all of the children in

this village who know me as the witch. I have no magical powers and no broomstick, no cauldron or book of spells. But I do have rather a lot of cats."

There was not a dry eye in the house. One by one, the audience rose to their feet, clapping and cheering. Alice-Miranda looked up at her friend. She hugged Miss Fayle, who hugged her right back.

And just in case you're wondering

S eptember Sykes eventually located her daughter, who was sobbing madly in the rose garden.
After a rather wild argument, they dashed straight
over to Winchesterfield-Downsfordvale and packed
Sloane's things. Within a week, the Sykeses' brand-
new house had a large For Sale sign in the front garden. September phoned Smedley in a terrible huff
but was soothed a little when he explained that his
offshore developing business wasn't faltering after
all. September told him that Sloane was being bul-
lied mercilessly at school, so she'd decided to sell the
house and the two of them were coming over to be

with him. She neglected to tell him about anything else that had happened.

Septimus steadfastly refused to leave school. He loved Fayle and Fayle loved him. Granny Henrietta heard all about what had happened. She'd always thought Septimus was just like his grandfather. She vowed to take care of him financially as long as he was at school or university, and in return, Septimus vowed to visit Granny Henrietta every week.

Caledonia Manor was transformed. Mr. Greening, Charlie, Wally and Hedges, with an army of students led by Alice-Miranda, had the garden looking shipshape in no time. Hugh Kennington-Jones was delighted to be able to send in the builders.

Henrietta moved back to Caledonia Manor to live with her sister. They had a nurse to take care of them, and a cook and housekeeper. Over time, they gained a lot more company. It was far too big a house for the two of them to rattle around in, so in honor of their great-great-grandfather Frederick Erasmus Fayle, Caledonia Manor became a training college for teachers. Alice-Miranda and her friends visited Granny Henrietta and Hephzibah at least once a week.

Miss Grimm and Professor Winterbottom declared the play a resounding success. Miss Reedy and Mr.

Lipp were already arguing over what they would put on next year.

Alice-Miranda thought long and hard about what had happened with the test papers and the Fayle School Charter. She decided that Sloane shouldn't be held accountable for the actions of her mother. So after much consideration and a long chat with Sep, Alice-Miranda decided to write to Sloane and see if she might like to be pen pals. After all, everyone deserves a second chance—don't they?

Cast of
Characters

THE HIGHTON-SMITH-KENNINGTON-JONES
HOUSEHOLD

Alice-Miranda Highton-Smith-Kennington-Jones	Only child, seven and a half years of age
Cecelia Highton-Smith	Alice-Miranda's doting mother
Hugh Kennington-Jones	Alice-Miranda's doting father
Aunt Charlotte Highton-Smith	Cecelia's younger sister
Lawrence Ridley	Famous movie actor and Aunt Charlotte's fiancé

Dolly Oliver	Family cook, part-time food technology scientist
Mrs. Shillingsworth	Head housekeeper
Mr. Greening	Gardener
Mrs. Maggie Greening	Mr. Greening's wife
Granny Bert (Albertine Rumble)	Former housekeeper at Highton Hall
Daisy Rumble	Granddaughter of Granny Bert, a maid at Highton Hall
Bonaparte	Alice-Miranda's pony
Max	Stablehand
Cyril	Helicopter pilot

FRIENDS OF THE HIGHTON-SMITH-KENNINGTON-JONES FAMILY

Aunty Gee	Granny Highton-Smith's best friend, Cecelia's godmother and the Queen
Prince Shivaji	Indian prince and friend of the family

WINCHESTERFIELD-DOWNSFORDVALE ACADEMY FOR PROPER YOUNG LADIES STAFF

Miss Ophelia Grimm	Headmistress
Aldous Grump	Miss Grimm's husband

Mrs. Louella Derby	Personal secretary to the headmistress
Miss Livinia Reedy	English teacher
Mr. Josiah Plumpton	Science teacher
Howie (Mrs. Howard)	House mistress
Mr. Cornelius Trout	Music teacher
Miss Benitha Wall	PE teacher
Cook (Mrs. Doreen Smith)	Cook
Charlie Weatherly (Mr. Charles)	Gardener
Wally Whitstable	Stablehand

STUDENTS

Millicent Jane McLoughlin-McTavish-McNoughton-McGill	Alice-Miranda's best friend and roommate
Jacinta Headlington-Bear	Talented gymnast, school's former second-best tantrum thrower and a friend
Danika Rigby	Head prefect
Madeline Bloom, Ivory Hicks, Ashima Divall, Lizzy Briggs, Shelby Shore, Susannah Dare	Friends
Sloane Sykes	New student

FAYLE SCHOOL FOR BOYS STAFF

Professor Wallace Winterbottom — Headmaster

Mrs. Deidre Winterbottom — Professor Winterbottom's wife

Miss Quigley — Personal assistant to the headmaster

Professor Herman Pluss — Mathematics teacher

Mr. Harold Lipp — English and drama teacher

Mr. Horatio Huntley — House master

Hedges — Gardener

Parsley — Professor Winterbottom's West Highland Terrier

STUDENTS

Lucas Nixon — Lawrence Ridley's son

Septimus Sykes — Brother of Sloane Sykes

OTHERS

September Sykes — Mother of Sloane and Septimus

Smedley Sykes — Father of Sloane and Septimus

Percy Sykes — Deceased grandfather of Sloane and Septimus

| Henrietta Sykes | Stepgranny of Sloane and Septimus |
| Matron Payne | Matron at the Golden Gates Retirement Home |

About the Author

Jacqueline Harvey has spent her working life teaching in girls' boarding schools. She's never met a witch in the woods, but she has come across quite a few girls who remind her a little of Alice-Miranda.

Jacqueline has published six novels for young readers in her native Australia. Her first picture book, *The Sound of the Sea,* was named a Children's Book Council of Australia Honor Book. She is currently working on Alice-Miranda's next adventure.

For more about Jacqueline and Alice-Miranda, go to:

www.alice-miranda.com

and

www.jacquelineharvey.com.au